# restored

## THE WALSH FAMILY

## KATE CANTERBARY

VESPER PRESS

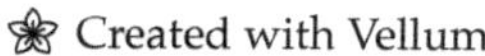 Created with Vellum

**Sam Walsh is ready to call himself a married man.**

He's finally put an end to decades of self-destruction and turned over a healthy new leaf. But love and marriage are only the beginning—and it's all about to get more complicated.

**Tiel Desai never planned on saying "I do" again.**

Before she can blink, she's swept up into a Walsh wedding whirlwind while also busy winning over her future in-laws, grappling with a bumpy adjustment to her new job, and keeping it together when a string of disappointments hit.

**They're trying to build a future but that means demolishing the past.**

They beat back their demons and learn to love each other through every season of life, but love might not be the solution to every problem that crawls their way.

CW: *Parent loss; chronic illness experienced by a main character; family abandonment experienced by a main character; infertility; pregnancy loss.*

CW: *Parent loss; chronic illness experienced by a main character; family abandonment experienced by a main character; infertility; pregnancy loss.*

*For the ones who put the baby shirts away.*

## MAY

I'D FORGOTTEN how the morning sun slanted through the old firehouse's windows and bathed Sam's bed in bright warmth.

It was intense, almost blinding, but I didn't want anything to change. I wanted to remember every ounce of this moment because nothing I'd experienced in the past three months came anywhere close to the level of perfection that was Sam's body wrapped around mine right now.

Not earning a doctorate.

Not convincing my twice-a-week guitar lesson, Seraphina, to tell me why she *loved* One Direction.

Not telling my sister to fuck off when she announced she had a baby girl and strongly suggested I move back to New Jersey to be her nanny.

Nothing was as perfect as having my precious, pervy boy back. Finally.

"You smell good," he murmured, his mountain man beard tickling my neck.

"I seriously doubt that," I said.

Sam shifted beside me and hooked his jean-covered thigh over my legs. He was still dressed—we both were—and part of me appreciated that I didn't need to be naked and naughty to feel this close to him. We both knew there was a lot to talk about, but when we'd arrived at the firehouse last night, we'd known there would be time for all the words later. Touching each other, resting our heads on the same pillow, just *being* together was what mattered then.

It was the best sleep I'd gotten in months.

"You're always saying that, but you smell like *you*, and I've missed *you* so much."

His words were muffled as he spoke against my skin, and while I wanted to ask whether smelling like me meant smelling like stale pepperoncini, his lips moved up my neck and I didn't want to think anymore. I urged him closer to me, pulling at his clothes until he was pressed against me and his mouth covered mine.

"I have to tell you," he said around a groan. "I have to tell you about something I—"

"Sam," I sighed.

I knew exactly where this was going. I knew Sam, and I knew these past three months were probably filled with his special brand of self-inflicted torture. If I was being honest with myself, I'd been doing the same thing.

"I screwed up," he said, his forehead pressed to mine. "So many things I should have done differently, but this…"

I searched his eyes, hoping to see what I needed there. "We were broken up," I said. "Whatever happened,

happened. What matters is that you're here now and we're moving past it."

"But—"

"You don't have to say anything else," I whispered. "We both screwed up. We were both wrong. We're going to make it work."

"I vomited on a woman," he said.

What else could I do but laugh? This was a story I needed to hear. "You what?"

He sighed and dropped his head to my shoulder. "A couple months ago, before leaving town, I went out and got really drunk. Really drunk. *Stupid* drunk. I had the brilliant idea to get loaded on shots and try to forget everything…" His voice trailed off and he glanced at me, his expression an uncomfortable blend of disgust and regret. "I let someone rub my dick and the whole time I was thinking about how the only thing I wanted was you, and then I puked on her."

I didn't like hearing about anyone touching Sam, but something about vomit interrupting a hand job was abso- lutely beautiful in every corner of karma. I knew Sam wasn't sitting at home and crying over his blueprints when we separated. He wasn't the kind of guy who wrote poetry or camped at a girl's door; he did reckless, self-destructive shit like this.

Or maybe that's who he *was*.

"A lot?"

This solid mass of man pinning me to the bed, he was new. It would take me weeks and months—years, even—to catalogue all the *new* and fold it into the complex symphony of Sam.

"Yes, Tiel, quite a bit," he said while I shook with laugh- ter. "I'm pleased you're finding this so funny. Here I am, thinking you're going to tear my balls off and shove them up my ass, and you're fucking laughing at me. That's splendid."

My fingernails scraped up his sides. "Would it make it better if I took off my shirt?"

Sam smiled, nodding, while I pulled the fabric over my head and unclasped my bra. He growled, and that was *it*—the single sound that plucked a chord deep inside me and roused all those dormant desires into frenetic awareness.

"I love you," he said as he lowered his head to my chest. "I love you." His lips moved to my nipple, drawing it into his mouth gently, softly. "I love you."

I dragged my fingers through his shaggy hair as I tangled my legs around his waist. "I love you, too."

His fingers trailed down my belly and flipped open the buttons on my jeans. His hand slipped inside, cupping me just enough that I felt bliss curling around my nerves and muscles.

"Sam? Sam? *Sam!*"

I heard sounds but couldn't place them in a rational order. The only things I cared about were Sam and the orgasm that was a second away from unraveling. It was a sensation I almost didn't recognize after spending the past three months drowning in coffee and music therapy research, but one I was damn pleased to encounter.

"Are you fucking serious? You come home and don't bother to fucking tell—*oh shit.*"

Suddenly, Sam's mouth left my breast and he was dragging the blanket over me. "Don't you ever knock, Riley?"

"Can you show me a door to knock, Sam?" Riley gestured around him.

This old firehouse was one wide-open space after

another, with the only form of room division coming from brick archways. One hundred years ago, the area Sam used as his bedroom housed thirty sets of bunk beds for the men who faced countless fires on the docks and nearby mills. I didn't have to know much more about the history or architecture of this odd building that Sam and Riley called home to know that constructing walls wouldn't feel right.

He jerked his chin in my direction, and despite his obvious exasperation with Sam, a sweet smile was tugging at his lips. "Hi, Tiel."

"Hi, Riley," I said, waving from under the blanket. "It's good to see you."

"You better *not* have seen anything!" Sam yelled.

"I didn't," Riley said. "And can we get back to the matter of you showing up here without so much as a text? What the fuck?"

Sam hauled me into his arms, his back to Riley. "I was ready," he said, gazing at me with a warm smile. Then he glanced to Riley. "Are you just getting home?"

"I crashed at Matt and Lauren's," he said. He leaned against the brick column, his ankles crossed and his arms folded over his chest as if he intended to stay and chat. "They've been inviting me over for dinner since you've been gone, and sometimes I've stayed there. Matt left for a run with Nick, and Lauren was going to yoga...but we're all having a cookout at Patrick and Andy's place tonight. You two should come."

He shifted his weight to his forearms, and shot a glance over his shoulder. "Listen, Ri. I haven't talked to more than one person at a time in three months. I need a slow reintroduction to society. A big event might short-circuit my brain."

"But sangria," Riley sang, his fingers splayed in the manliest version of jazz hands I'd ever seen. "Everyone loves sangria. Andy puts something in it that's voodoo-magic good."

Sam shifted, bringing me closer to him and blocking everything from my line of sight except his body. And mother of pearls, there was a lot to love. He'd always tended toward lean and strong, but now he was *fit*. Thick in all the right spots, trim in others. A tan lingered around his shoulders and arms, and his once perfectly sculpted hair was wild and overgrown. But it wasn't the outside that stirred me. It was the complex mind and tender heart, and I wanted to own a spot in both.

"I haven't had a drink since that night at Alibi," he said, turning a meaningful stare in my direction. That must have been the scene of the dick-petting-and-vomiting incident, and yeah, we'd be avoiding that venue for a bit. "I want to see everyone, but we also need some time today, just the two of us."

"I'm gonna leave now because I'm pretty sure I'm not one of the two you have in mind," Riley called, but I couldn't see over Sam's obscenely broad shoulders and only murmured in response. "But I want you both washed, clothed, and ready to roll by seven tonight. We're going to this fucking barbeque, and you're going to enjoy it, too."

"That will be interesting, Sunshine." Sam turned to me, a quiet laugh bubbling up from his chest.

"I'm walking away," Riley shouted.

"Walk faster," Sam yelled.

"All of this is going to be interesting, Sam," I said. "All of it."

He burrowed into the crook of my neck and his mouth

found my skin, and I pulled him to me, craving more, wanting his weight pressing down on me. I needed to lick him, bite him, kiss him, hold him, claim him. I needed to fill my hands with every little thing I could offer, and beg him to take me as I came and promise to give him anything, everything.

"We're going to make it work. We're going to figure it out," he said, and he was close enough for me to feel each word on my skin. He pushed my jeans over my hips, and together we shoved them down my legs. I was nodding, humming and murmuring in agreement, fucking *trembling* for him as I attacked his belt buckle. "*Tell me*, Tiel. Tell me we're gonna last because I can't have you right now if this isn't real."

"It's real," I said. "We're real."

It was such a damn victory to get his jeans off that I flung them clear across the room. There was a shuffle for condoms, detaching his glucose monitor, tossing extraneous pillows to the floor, but then, *finally*, he was inside me. He was moving and wrapping me up in his arms, anchoring himself while he spoke in broken pleas and demands against my skin.

*Ah, Tiel, I want*

*I need*

*Wrap your legs around*

*Fucking flex your little pussy like that again and this will be over fast*

*Yes, baby, take it* all

*I want to hear you*

*Oh, fuck*

*Tell me how good my cock is for you*

Sam was rough and wild, and sweet in all the ways that I needed. That I'd missed.

He held me with all the love and adoration he could gather into a single embrace, and he fucked me like he was conquering a village.

# Part One

LOVE...

*One*

SAM

*November*

TIEL LEANED INTO ME, nodding toward the kitchen, and whispered, "You ready?"

I blew out a long breath and frowned. Riley was seated at the table, the sports section of the newspaper spread out before him. He was eating cereal out of a two-quart mixing bowl, and he was naked save for his Batman boxers.

"Can we wait until he's clothed?" I asked. His dress shirt, tie, and khakis were hanging off the back of the chair to his right. "I mean, I know we see his dick a lot—"

"*A lot*," Tiel murmured, her lips pursing.

"Yeah, I don't enjoy knowing that you can draw it from memory, sweetheart," I said, exasperated. My brother preferred loincloth living, and my patience for that was waning.

"Come on," she said, tangling her fingers with mine.

My thumb traced the hard lines of her ring. Her *engage-*

*ment* ring. It had only been seated at that spot for twenty-four hours, and I was still high on the primal thrill of conquest.

She chose *me*, she wanted *me*, she was keeping *me*.

"The deal was we tell Riley before we tell the rest of your family, and then we tell *my* family, although I still contend they'll say something offensive about the Irish but otherwise not be able to find a single shit to give. Actually," she said with a heavy sigh, "I don't think we should bother telling my parents anything. Send them an invite, and be shocked if they show up."

"That's not one of the options," I said.

Riley growled at the newspaper and muttered, "Those motherfuckers need to get their offensive line together," before refilling his bowl.

"He's like our first baby," she said, dropping her head to my chest. "We're getting real parenting experience. From a twenty-eight year old."

"Well..." I was about to protest that Riley often appointed himself as den mother and had done a decent job of looking after me when I'd refused to look after myself, but then he spilled milk all over his bare chest and mopped it up with his tie.

I rubbed my knuckles down her belly. "I've got time if you want to work on our *next* baby."

She dipped her chin, smiling. "We worked pretty hard yesterday," she said. "I'd be surprised if you didn't get the job done."

*This.*

I wanted this. I wanted to stop talking about starting a family *someday* and make it a reality *today.*

It was one of the most ridiculous thoughts living in my

head—and I had a lot of fucking odd thoughts up there—because I'd never imagined this for myself. Under no construct had my future ever included a wife, children, or anything beyond functional alcoholism and a thinly leashed contempt for the universe as I knew it.

But I had a recurring vision of Tiel teaching our babies music. Us going camping and fishing with our kids. Our little family eating dinner and celebrating holidays around the table I built. And I wanted those visions to be real.

We'd stopped using condoms after a long weekend away when we each thought the other packed them, and Tiel went on a rant about hating how they made her hands smell like old tires. There was also a talk about how we were a little obsessed with each other, and wanted to be together for always, and we wanted some tiny humans in our lives. Maybe a lot of tiny humans.

"I'm very goal-oriented. You give me a target and I'll hit it," I said.

"Oh, you *hit it* all right," she said with a snort.

"When will we, uh…" I cleared my throat. She didn't love it when I asked about these things. "When will we know?"

Tiel studied my tie, her bottom lip wiggling between her teeth. "Two weeks, or so." She looked up at me. "After yesterday, I'm thinking it's a sure thing."

I didn't ask why yesterday was any different from the past two months, instead bending to kiss my fiancée's forehead. "Just wait until tonight. Maybe you should clear your schedule for the week. Rest up. Let me hit the target some more."

"Let's not forget about all the meetings I have, or all the

journal articles I have to finish, or the classes I have to teach."

The excitement in her eyes dimmed, but she quickly blinked it away as if she could hide her frustration from me. She didn't love her new job as an associate professor of music therapy, and though she hadn't come out and said it yet, it was the worst-kept secret in the home we shared with Riley.

There were times when I'd find her sitting in the firehouse's old communal showers-turned-studio, staring at her instruments or sheet music with none of the hunger and passion I'd once seen from her. It started shortly after she moved in here, and there was a period of time when I attributed her unease to me, and our new living arrangement. But I learned that my free-spirited girl liked this taste of the settled life, and it didn't take long to map the crests and crashes of her moods to her gig in academia.

She'd bring it up when she was ready, and I wasn't meant to rush her.

"But seriously, I'm a sure thing," she said. She held up her hand, inclining her head toward the pink diamond ring. "You can retire the pick-up lines now."

Her hand wrapped around my belt, she dragged me into the kitchen and pointed to a chair across from Riley. He looked up with a quick nod, and promptly returned to his sports page. He hated reading—always had—but he was devoted to his New England teams and didn't enjoy interruptions to his daily study of the stats.

Also, he wasn't a morning person. He didn't start speaking in complete sentences until shortly before lunch, and even then, it was limited to discussions of food.

Tiel set a spinach-papaya-cucumber smoothie beside

me, and sat down with a bagel and jar of cream cheese in hand. Riley acknowledged her with a jut of his chin, and she said, "He put a ring on it."

"That's awesome," Riley said, the sleepy fog clearing from his eyes and his face breaking into a wide smile. "Awesome, just awesome. Everyone's getting married around here."

I was about to agree when Tiel said, "Wait. What? Did I miss something?"

Riley blinked to the side, his mouth open as if words were stuck on his tongue. "No. Right," he said. "Matt and Lauren, and now you guys. That's it. No one else. My bad."

Tiel and I glanced at each other, confused.

"Riley," she started, "is there something you're not telling us?" He shook his head vigorously. "Are *you* seeing someone?"

He shoved the spoon in his mouth and shook his head again. "No," he said around his cereal. "I'm not ready or looking for a commitment right now. I'm working on myself."

Tiel turned to face me. "Did he learn that line from you?"

"If he did, he didn't learn it recently," I scoffed.

"You didn't actually answer that question, Riley. So… you're not seeing anyone?" she asked. "Nothing casual? Not even a friend with benefits? None of that?"

"No," Riley said. "I was with one chick on and off through college, but she was fucking crazy. I mean, *fucking crazy*. Art chicks are freaky. Like outdoor cats. I've been a lone wolf since Dorrance."

"Outdoor cat?" Tiel said. "I don't understand that reference."

"Dorrance?" I repeated.

"Middle name," Riley said. "Her first name's Kacie, but she started going by her middle name when she got to art school. Like I said, outdoor cat."

"What's an outdoor cat?" Tiel said.

"What about the dominatrix?" I asked. "That lasted a while."

"The *dominatrix*?" Tiel repeated. "No, forget the cat, I want to hear about *that*."

Riley shrugged as he dug into his cereal. "Met a woman at a deli. Turned out she was a dominatrix. Who knew?" He pointed his spoon at Tiel. "I learned a lot, but it wasn't my scene."

Tiel laughed as she smeared cream cheese over a chunk of bagel. "All for the research?"

Riley stared at his bowl, thinking before he replied, "It was cool at first, but like I said…not my scene."

"You can't leave it at that," Tiel said. "Come on. This is a safe space. We're in the trust tree here."

I glanced to Tiel. "Is that what we're calling this place now?"

She jerked a shoulder, a smile lifting her eyes. "That's what I'm calling it, yeah."

Riley refilled his cereal, and waved his spoon at Tiel again. "Mila came at me with a big purple strap-on, told me to suck her dick, and the only thing I could think of was Shannon. So that was traumatic. I safe-worded my ass right out of there, and never went back." He frowned and glanced away. "Oh, shit, I'm not supposed to say her name."

He knocked his fist against his forehead several times while Tiel layered both hands over her mouth to keep from laughing.

"Trust tree," I said. "It stays in the trust tree."

Riley glanced up with a quick nod and returned to his breakfast. "Yeah, well, she…Ma'am…texts me every now and then. Invites me to play. But…she has too many rules and obviously, I never remembered them, and that experience reminded me that I don't enjoy having my ass whipped. I have enough problems without pretending to like ritualistic beatings."

"This has been really informative," Tiel murmured. "You think you know someone, and then… Are you okay? I feel like I should hug you now."

"Nah, it's all good. When's the wedding?" Riley asked around another mouthful of cereal. He shot a glance at Tiel. "You should know we all get into a lot of trouble at weddings. Epic trouble."

I pushed away from the table to rinse out the smoothie jar. "I think you're exaggerating," I groaned from the sink.

"And I think I'm holding the chips on more wedding night shenanigans than you can imagine," Riley said. "You're kidding yourself if you think shenanigans won't go down at your wedding. Fixing old houses and fucking up shit at weddings. It's what the Walsh kids do."

---

GROWING UP IN A LOUD, meddlesome family of six, and then choosing to work with that same family, I'd always leaned toward keeping what personal information I had left to myself. It was never about secrecy, rather the persistent need to designate something as my own. When so much existed under the umbrella of communal property, that which only I owned was treasured.

And for the past year, the treasure was Tiel.

Keeping her to myself was entirely for my benefit. She joined my brother Matt's wife, Lauren, and my brother Patrick's girlfriend, Andy, for brunch sometimes, and had drinks with my sister Shannon when their schedules aligned, and Riley begged for her homemade Greek meatballs weekly, but she was still *mine*. She didn't belong to all of us the way Lauren or Andy or Matt's marathon buddy, Nick, did, and I was selfish enough to prefer that.

But the status quo was going to change. Marriage meant change, and deep down I knew I wanted the family I made with Tiel to be part of this bigger, messier, noisier family, too. However, I still needed to protect her from the thundering herd of well-dressed beasts known as my siblings.

I girded myself for this change as we reached the tail end of our Monday morning status meeting. We did this every week: everyone around the table in our Beacon Hill office's attic conference room, all our sustainable preservation projects on the table for review, and without fail, at least ten minutes devolved into family talk.

It was go time.

"Tiel and I are getting married," I announced.

I smiled to myself while I fished my phone from my suit coat pocket. I tapped the screen, and an image of Tiel and me appeared. It still seemed unbelievable that I was going to marry this girl.

Everyone crowded around me, offering handshakes and hugs, congratulations and quips about Tiel making an honest man out of me. But Shannon was still seated, watching while Andy and my brothers offered their well wishes.

I looked up and met Shannon's eyes across the table, and I couldn't believe she was still angry at me for taking time away from the office, and that she still held Tiel responsible for that sabbatical. She couldn't accept that I'd needed the time to get my shit in order, that I'd needed to make sense of my life, that I'd needed to be really fucking alone for a little while. She couldn't comprehend that leaving was about *me*, not about Tiel, not about her.

"Shannon?"

Her expression shifted into a perfect mask of hollow happiness. It was almost humorous how hard she worked at pretending she wasn't completely fucked up. It was no secret that Something Happened—something more than being pissed at me for falling off the face of the earth for a couple of months—but every time someone asked, Shannon blinked, smiled, and rattled off assorted details about diffi-cult negotiations or jogging some extra miles. She was laboring under the assumption that we hadn't noticed her clothes hanging off her small frame, or couldn't see deep bags under her eyes or the lonely cocktail of sadness, anger, and regret radiating from her.

"Congratulations!" she said eventually, rounding the table to wrap me in a bony hug. She felt like she was trying to disappear. "Have you set a date yet?"

I dropped my hand to her shoulder, swallowing my annoyance, and shook my head. I wanted her to freak out the way she did when Matt got engaged, and tackle Tiel and me in a screaming hug, and then yell at us for making her cry. I didn't want the boss lady right now.

"No, we didn't get that far yesterday," I said.

"Well, there's a ton to plan," she said. Her expression turned serious, and she collected her things before retreating to the staircase. I'd put money on her returning to her office and making some phone calls to get available dates for the event space at Sixty State Street.

It was like she'd forgotten how to feel anything.

Shannon gestured toward me, another stiff smile in place, and she said, "We should get dinner soon, the three of us, and start thinking about dates, venues, themes. So much to do. Colors. Flowers. Everything. Let me know what works for you two, and we'll get together."

Her heels clacking against the stone staircase echoed after her, and the conference room was silent for a long moment.

I turned back to my siblings and Andy, my hands spread out before me.

"Please tell me you all saw that," I said. "Please tell me someone saw her run out of here like she was being chased by Death Eaters."

"We need to give her space," Patrick said.

"I'm tired of her being pissed at me and taking it out on Tiel," I said.

"We have been over this before, Sam. Not everything is about you. She's had a rough few months," Andy said. "She doesn't want to talk about it. She'll avoid the shit out of you if you don't play by the rules. I mean, Lauren pushed her hard, and Shannon barely talks to her now."

"Truth," Matt said. "My wife is very unhappy about the state of affairs."

"And it's not like you haven't done the exact same thing before," Riley muttered. "No. Strike that. You're a little more Wicked Witch of the West with your exits."

"Are you fucking kidding me?" I yelled. "I'm going down there and—"

"Don't," Riley interrupted. "Whatever you're thinking

right now, don't." He dropped a hand to my shoulder and pushed me into a chair.

I glanced at Patrick. "Do you need anything else from me this morning?"

He lowered his laptop screen with a long sigh. "Congratulations, man. We're happy for you," he said. "But please don't upset her. I have too much on my plate today for another round of Shannon staring out the window and pretending she's not crying."

I collected my things and moved toward the staircase. "It's truly comical how you're all so concerned about Shannon right now, but none of you motherfuckers had noticed anything was wrong until I came home last spring and pointed it out to you. It's also amusing that you think we should simply leave her alone and hope that whatever is slowly killing her magically disappears. If it was any one of us, Shannon wouldn't let that shit fly."

I didn't wait to hear their disagreement. I headed straight for Shannon's office and silenced her assistant, Tom, with a sharp glare as I passed his desk.

Where most people avoided confrontation, Shannon thrived on it. She was born for argument, negotiation, cross-examination. She held nothing back, and when it came to personal matters, it was where she was most honest.

I was praying that bringing this confrontation to her door didn't push her over the edge.

"Is there something you wish to share with me?" I asked.

I dropped into a chair and waited for her to acknowledge me. Her elbows were propped on the desk and her head was in her hands, and though I'd seen her in that pose plenty of times, this moment was scented with bitterness and loss.

"No," she said, shaking out her hair. "A lot on my mind today. A lot of meetings. You know how it is. Mondays are always crazy."

Shannon was good with poker faces. Really good. But she was failing right now. "You're falling apart," I murmured. "Could we drop the 'everything's okay' act?"

"And I'm checking out two more properties this afternoon," she continued, ignoring me. "A pair of brownstones that were in the process of being remodeled but the developer ran out of cash so they've been vacant for a few years. Could be interesting."

"If I wanted your schedule, I could have asked Tom. Why don't you cut the shit and tell me what's going on?"

She stared at her skirt. "Nothing is going on. I'm thrilled for you, truly, and will do anything to help with planning the wedding," she said, and it sounded like a well-rehearsed line.

"That's a load of bullshit," I said, and her gaze snapped to mine, shocked. "It's bullshit. You should have seen your face up there, Shan. You were devastated, and I want to know why."

"Not devastated," she said. "Just surprised. It seems like you just moved in together, and..." She stared at her fingernails for a minute before heaving out a sigh and continuing, "And I can't wait to help with the planning. You're thinking summer, right? Summer weddings are wonderful, though the best spots book up quickly. What about The Cliff House in Ogunquit? Or were you thinking somewhere in town?"

She babbled on, rattling off the names of every hot wedding location in the region and conducting a debate with herself about which location I'd prefer.

"Shannon." I edged forward, into her line of sight. "Stop

it. Do not handle me. Do not spin this conversation. If you have a problem that you need to get off your chest, you need to get it out or get over it right now."

She went back to staring at her fingers, and minutes passed without any indication she'd heard me.

"That's not it," she finally said. "Not at all. I know it's selfish, and I'm sorry, but...I wish you'd called me. I wish you'd told me as soon as it happened. I wish you'd asked me to go ring shopping with you."

I swallowed a sigh and sat back in the seat. The first thing I thought when I saw that ring was that I wanted it for Tiel. The second thought was along the lines of "Oh holy fuck, I want to marry this girl." The third thought was deep, organ-twisting regret that Shannon wasn't there with me. We'd always been close, and done everything together, but right now we were miles apart.

"I didn't exactly plan it out. I didn't intentionally exclude you. And yesterday, well, we got a little carried away."

"I'm happy for you and Tiel. Really. Now when can we get together to celebrate? I'll bring the champagne," she said.

"Soon, but..." I started, "I love you. You know that."

Shannon jerked a shoulder up in agreement, and gestured for me to continue. She wanted this discussion over, and she wanted to move on to tasks and projects where she didn't have to deal with whichever gray area was dragging her down.

"But that doesn't mean you can adopt our wedding as your new pet project," I said.

I had to rip the bandage, the same way she'd ripped it for me in the past. It was going to hurt, and she was going to hate me, but I had to snap Shannon out of this fog *and* shield Tiel from Shannon's war-general brand of event planning.

"You hijacked Matt and Lauren's wedding, but they were too busy to care," I said, laughing.

Shannon's glare was a clear indication that she found no humor in this statement.

"We want to do this our own way. Tiel will reach out to you, I can guarantee that, but she'll do it on her time. She adores you, and I really appreciate how you've given her as much time as she needed to warm up to you, and everyone else. But that doesn't mean you can smother her now."

Her eyebrows knit together, and she pursed her lips for a long pause before responding. "I wasn't trying to hijack anything. It's your day, and I just wanted to help with—"

"Give Tiel some space," I pleaded. She'd been working on a relationship with Shannon since the summer, but wedding planning resided in a much higher weight class than weeknight drinks and pedicures. "If she wants your opinion on these things, she'll ask. Until then, I need you to take an enormous step back."

Her bottom lip quivered for a moment before she snared it between her teeth, and she nodded, the fight abandoning her. She wasn't stepping up for this confrontation.

"Of course, Sam. Whatever you need. If there's anything at all that I can do for either of you, just let me know."

---

**"YOU SAID *WHAT* TO SHANNON?"** Tiel cried.

"I told her to back off," I said as I wiped my hands on a kitchen towel. "What's wrong with that?"

Tiel shook her head and muttered at the pot on the stove. "Okay, let's see. Where should I start? How about your sister already thinks I'm an enormous bitch? Or that I have to plan out what I'll say to her before I see her so that I don't have a fit of word vomit? Or that she's going through a rough patch? Or that I've spent, hmm…" She held up her fingers as she ticked off the months. "May, June, July, August, September, October, and November. Yep, that's seven months. I've spent seven months trying to make friends with your sister, and Andy and Lauren, too, and then you kill it all in one morning."

"She needed to hear it," I said.

Tiel leaned against the countertop, groaning. "In summary, the only people excited to hear that we're engaged are Riley and Ellie. Outstanding."

She crossed her arms over her chest, her fingertips tapping out a beat on her elbow. I let the music in her mind take over rather than inquiring further into her best friend's reaction. I'd texted Ellie a picture of the ring and asked for her blessing last week. It made perfect sense to me. She was Tiel's only true guardian, and if there was anyone I needed on my side, it was Miz Ellie Tsai.

She'd sent me a link to a music video—'Everlasting Light' by The Black Keys'—and I'd interpreted that as her stamp of approval.

Tiel started pacing around the kitchen, keeping her hands busy by sorting mail and drying dishes. She wasn't one to sit still for long. "Did you talk to Erin?"

I studied the grill pan for a long moment before turning to meet her eyes. My youngest sibling didn't do phone calls, ever. Her lifestyle could also be fairly encapsulated as "professional backpacking through Europe."

"I emailed her. I haven't heard back yet, but that's not unusual for her."

Tiel sighed into the refrigerator as she reached for the wine. She'd departed from her preference for craft beers, and somewhere in recent months adopted a taste for Riesling and pinot grigio, but calling that out didn't figure into the complete and total honesty agreement we'd enacted.

We'd scheduled time for a Serious Conversation one weekend in July, and set the stakes high: no sex until the big topics were suitably addressed. All of the cards were on the table, and we talked through everything from my father's unrepentantly awful stamp on me and my siblings to her trust and abandonment issues to all of the small things that drove us crazy. There was a lot of baggage to process—we maintained a running joke that neither of us packed light— and none of these topics made for easy conversation. It was akin to passing through airport security, with your belongings moving through an X-ray machine, your body open for intimate inspection, and your pants seconds from falling down.

But we'd survived, and before sunset that Sunday, I was buried inside her.

"I'm sorry that I upset you, but Shannon needs a hard shove. She's wasting away in front of our eyes, and everyone is acting like we should watch quietly while it happens."

"I think you've forgotten how a bad breakup can wreck your life," Tiel said. "She's working herself into the ground and shutting everyone out because it's her way of grieving and coping. Stop instigating arguments with her, and tell her it's okay to feel her feelings."

"Breakup? This is about a guy?" I asked. "When? Who? No one told me."

Tiel brought her hands to my face and tugged me down for a quick kiss. "How can you be so smart and so clueless at the same time?"

"It's one of my many gifts and talents," I said.

Things got rockier after my chat with Shannon. Lauren —sweet, loving Miss Honey—called this afternoon to bust my balls about hearing the news from Matt, and not directly from me. She seemed genuinely hurt by the implication that she didn't rank high enough in my book to warrant telling her myself, and that was when I started feeling like the highest grade of asshole possible.

Or the lowest. Whichever was worse.

Riley piled on with a lecture that bordered on beat down over my discussion with Shannon. He heard about it from Tom, of course. He also felt it was necessary to remind me that she was dealing with some shit, and if I couldn't say anything nice to her, I wasn't to say anything at all.

Then, Tiel and I called her parents. Or, more accurately, Tiel called, and I listened while her parents talked over each other about her older sister, Agapi, for twenty-five minutes. They were especially pleased with Agapi for doing something miraculous with menus at the Greek restaurant they owned, and her husband was "a doll," and her infant daughter, Anatola, was the most beautiful, brilliant child ever conceived. Once Agapi Appreciation Hour was over, they turned their attention to Tiel.

I knew she spoke with her father about once a month, and she'd mentioned she was seeing someone, but she'd erred on the side of sharing less and I respected that choice.

Her family situation was far too complicated for me to jump in and demand higher billing before our engagement.

When they started with their questions about whether she had a job or a place to stay, I understood why she kept these calls to a minimum. I also wanted to make sure they grasped how wrong they were about her, but her stern expression told me to stay quiet. I didn't correct their faulty assumptions, but I did growl like an irritable wolf when they invited her to "move home and start over" whenever she was ready. For some incomprehensible reason, her parents treated her prodigy-level musical talent as a burden and embarrassment.

It made no fucking sense, but who was I to point out family dysfunction?

When she announced we were engaged, there was thirty seconds of dead silence. Their disapproval dripped from every word and stilted pause, and though I still didn't grasp why they were such dickheads, I knew it was another reminder that it was time for us to shake off the dead weights of the past and build our own family.

"This is not something we're going to stress out about," I said as I moved salmon and vegetables around the grill pan. "And please clarify for me why the hell we should care what anyone thinks anyway? We're happy for us, and everyone else can fuck off."

"You don't actually believe that," she said. "The everyone fucking off part."

"I mostly do," I said. "We're going to do what makes us happy. End of story."

Tiel grabbed a set of plates and silverware and busied herself at the table. "Sam," she said, shaking her head. "You know that's not even close to the end of the story. We don't get to live happily ever after just yet. Simply because we want to get married doesn't mean that we won't deal with real life and real issues."

Recognizing she was right, I didn't say anything else as I headed toward the table.

Tiel looked around the kitchen and great room, her eyes narrowed. "Is Riley not joining us? I mean, there's food on the table and he's not here, and I can't remember a time when that's ever happened."

"The Patriots are playing in Foxboro tonight," I said as I passed Tiel a bowl of veggies. "Magnolia has season tickets."

Her eyes widened as she chuckled. "Ah, yes. His *bro*, Magnolia."

"Yeah," I murmured.

Talking about Magnolia, the landscape architect whose romantic advances I'd missed for months until she took it upon herself to kiss me while Tiel watched last winter, was akin to handling a live grenade. No matter what I did, it was ending with an explosion.

And to add a little extra boom to that explosion, Magnolia and Riley had bonded over their shared love of New England sports. If they weren't cheering on their favorite teams from the sidelines, they were doing it at Boston's best taverns and pubs. He insisted their relationship was strictly platonic, and he seized every opportunity to remind me that the disaster with Magnolia was all my fault. He didn't see any reason to refuse forty-yard-line seats because I was deaf to shameless flirting.

It wasn't that Tiel was dwelling on my massive cock-up with Magnolia. But there was some truth to the old adage about letting things heal by leaving them alone. The constant presence of Magnolia—even if only in Riley's outings and her work on the Turlan project—wore at the wound.

When we finished eating, I refilled Tiel's wine glass and elected to dive back into wedding talk. "Forget your parents, forget my siblings, forget everything," I said, wise enough not to drop Magnolia's name twice in one evening. "Tiel. I want to be married to you. I want to be yours, and I want you as mine. This is about us, and nothing else. Please, sweetheart, let's pick a date, and then we focus on the important things, like honeymoon destinations and what to name our kids."

She smiled and set her glass down, then rounded the table to nestle on my lap. Her hair was cut short, just barely brushing her shoulders, and as I buried my face there, I was hit with the delicate aroma of her shampoo. My lips trailed over her neck and collarbone, and my arms roped around her waist. There was something about her skin, her scent, her smile that grounded me.

"You and your smooth lines," she said, pulling her phone from her back pocket. "Let's take a look at—oh. Huh."

I glanced to Tiel and then her phone's screen, and found her staring at a message. "What is it?"

"An email from my father." She dragged her bottom lip between her teeth before continuing. "They—my parents—want us to spend Thanksgiving with them. They...they're looking forward to meeting you."

I murmured in agreement, although the sound was something closer to a dubious grunt. These people had been horrible to Tiel. This evening's phone call only validated my opinion.

But they were still family, and it was Tiel's decision how we proceeded.

Her thumb passed over the screen as she reread the message several times, her brow wrinkled and her lips pressed tight, and I wanted to take it all away for her. I wanted to save her the agony of grappling with a toxic relationship, and I wanted to shield her from the pain that would eventually come from it. I was optimistic about many things, but a sudden about-face from the parents who'd treated Tiel like a second-class citizen her entire life wasn't one of them. Regardless of what she decided, she'd end up hurt.

"What do you want to do, Sunshine?"

She set her phone on the table with a decisive nod. "I want to go upstairs and get out of these clothes, and then I want to listen to some Van Morrison while you do perverted things to me, and I don't want to talk about any of this stuff. Not tonight, and maybe not for a few days. Is that okay?"

"Sweetheart, I am committed to loving you, honoring you, and fucking you senseless any time you want." I nodded toward the staircase. "Be naked when I get up there."

*November*

**Sam:** I'm finished with this. I'm going to sit him down today and tell him he needs to go
**Tiel:** NO! no no no no no
**Sam:** I'm serious
**Sam:** The kid is a fucking menace and him living on his own wouldn't be the worst thing to ever happen
**Tiel:** You are not kicking Riley out
**Sam:** Did he or did he not walk in while you were riding me this morning and therefore, see you naked?
**Tiel:** He didn't see anything
**Sam:** We need our own space
**Tiel:** He's like a baby bird. We can't kick him out of the nest
**Sam:** I'd like to fuck my fiancée without an audience
**Tiel:** Then get better at locking doors, babe.
**Sam:** I'm still adjusting to the fact we *have* doors

**Sam:** Also – it's not like we can just kick that thing shut. It's an actual barn door, sweetheart.

**Tiel:** If it's too difficult…maybe we shouldn't have sex every morning. We can cut back. Just a thought.

**Sam:** Okay. All right. We're not kicking Riley out.

**Tiel:** See? That wasn't so hard.

**Tiel:** And please stop threatening to make him leave. That makes me really sad.

**Tiel:** He's always been nice to me and he loves my meatballs

**Sam:** I love your meatballs too

**Tiel:** It sounds dirty when you say it

**Sam:** While that might be true, how long are we supposed to keep him around?

**Tiel:** Why do we have to set an expiration date? he's part of our family

**Sam:** Because he walks in on us when we're having sex!

**Sam:** And sometimes I think he won't take the next step unless I force him. If I hadn't left him in charge of the Turlan project, he'd still be running permits and doing basic intern tasks.

**Sam:** It's his really fucked up form of self-preservation.

**Tiel:** Ahem

**Sam:** I know, I'm the last one to criticize anyone's coping mechanisms

**Sam:** But it's preservation. That's all it is. He can't fuck up if he doesn't do anything

**Sam:** When this Turlan project is done, he's going to be the hottest young architect on the east coast. He's going to have more work than he knows what to do with, and it's because he's doing an amazing fucking job

**Sam:** But he has to get out of his own way

**Tiel:** Have you told him that?

**Sam:** I've certainly tried and he's done his damnedest to blow it off

**Tiel:** Perhaps we can help him find his work wings, but keep him in the nest at home

**Sam:** If he's living with us and eating cereal in his underwear when he's 45, we're revisiting my original proposal

**Tiel:** Deal, but I'll probably lobby hard to keep him then, too.

---

**Sam:** Thank you

**Tiel:** ???

**Sam:** Just opened my laptop and found your note.

**Tiel:** You're my favorite and I wanted you to know

**Sam:** Did you also want me to spend 15 minutes cooling off on the roof deck? Because you succeeded with your little "requests" for tonight. I had to walk out of a meeting with Patrick and Riley

**Tiel:** Sounds like a lovely consequence

**Sam:** You're my favorite, too

---

**Tiel:** I'm meeting Lauren and Andy for pedicures tonight

**Tiel:** Do you know if Shannon will be there? I've texted her but haven't heard back

**Tiel:** Probably because SOMEONE told her to get lost and never talk to me again

**Sam:** Sorry sweetheart, I was meeting with clients and Matt got a little fanatical about foundations and retaining walls.

Long story short, we're rebuilding both and he needs to keep his geek leashed.

**Sam:** I haven't seen Shan all day, and that was not what I said to her.

**Tiel:** It was the gist.

**Sam:** I do not enjoy arguing with my fiancée so I will not say anything further

**Sam:** Text me when you're finished with your pedicure and I'll pick you up.

**Tiel:** Thank you. maybe we can get tacos and sort out the stuff that I've been avoiding all week?

**Sam:** Tacos: yes. Stuff you're avoiding: only if you're ready and want to.

---

"OH, let me see, let me see," Lauren squealed from across the pedicure spa. She'd caught Andy examining my ring when she arrived—I'd never before been so aware of my chipped nail polish and violin string-calloused fingers— and immediately made her way toward us while also trying to unbuckle her heels.

"It's lovely," Andy said, glancing up at me with one of those half smiles that I was now interpreting as her version of glee. "I'm thrilled for you, and Sam."

She was a tough nut to crack, but the more time I spent with her, the more I admired her. She was calm and intelligent, and though she didn't say much, she was always genuine and kind to me. When Sam and I reunited after his time in Maine, I knew I had to salvage my relationships with his siblings and their significant others, and I figured they were going to make me work for it.

I was wrong.

The day after Sam and I started over, we went to a barbeque at Patrick and Andy's apartment. I was actually shaking in my sandals and terror-sweating like a beast, but Andy welcomed me into her home, hugged me, and then put me on fruit salad prep in the kitchen. I ended up pulling her aside after many glasses of sangria and apologizing for all of my prior offenses and extreme displays of awkwardness.

She shrugged it off, confided that she had plenty of her own awkward, and told me to get my ass to pedicure night or weekend brunch on the regular. That single, sloppy interaction shed light on the real Andy, the one I'd missed the first time around. The same went for Lauren, but I hadn't gained much traction with Shannon yet.

"Thank you, and—oh!" Lauren's arms closed around my shoulders, and for a small woman, she was alarmingly strong.

"It's so good to see you!" she cried, squeezing me tighter. "And you're getting married!"

I gulped back the flare of panic that shot up every time I heard those words. The panic had roared to life after that call with my parents. They didn't come out and say that I'd failed before, or that I was missing something essential to growing a healthy marriage, but their silence said everything.

And it wasn't a matter of cold feet for me. I wanted this, I wanted to make it work, and I wanted to quiet the doubt in my mind, but I couldn't erase the thorny fear that I'd never be enough for Sam.

It was like those signs at amusement parks that read "You Must Be This Tall To Ride," and I didn't measure up.

"I'm so excited. It's amazing," I said, emotion ringing in my voice. "And overwhelming."

Lauren offered a knowing nod, and gestured toward the bank of massaging pedicure chairs. "Let's sit down and get you a drink. You're engaged, which means everyone is up in your business and you deserve a steady stream of hard liquor."

"Shannon couldn't make it?" I asked.

Andy and Lauren exchanged a long, loaded glance before Andy said, "She was still at the office when I left."

Thanks to a certain fiancé, she was probably avoiding me.

"All right," Lauren said, holding up her hands. "This is what we're going to do. If she tries dodging us again, I'm going to that little ginger's office and dragging her out by her Burberry scarf."

"She's avoiding you, too?" I said.

At the same time, Andy said, "You're a lot braver than you look, Miss Honey."

"We are *not* devoting an entire drunk pedicure night to talking about how I'm going to take on the Black Widow and win," Lauren said, reaching over to grab my wrist. "Let's talk about pretty things. Show me that ring again."

Before we could delve any further into Shannon's apparent refusal to see any of us, Lauren launched straight into a detailed accounting of Matt's proposal two years ago, their holiday trip to Mexico where they surprised her parents with the news, and their wedding planning activities. It was good to hear about their struggles and stresses, and it was a sharp reminder that Lauren wasn't the annoyingly perfect Barbie doll that I pegged her for when we first met.

"I probably looked at five thousand dresses before I picked one," Lauren said. "I went to every shop in the state, and almost went to New York. I had dozens of bridal magazines and designers' catalogs, and hundreds of pins on my Pinterest board, but I couldn't work up more than a 'meh' for any of them. I couldn't decide on anything, and I remember calling my mother one afternoon and having an enormous meltdown. I thought my wedding was doomed. I thought there was something wrong with me because I wasn't finding The One."

Andy laughed into her margarita glass. "You tell that story with more angst than when Frodo Baggins tells the story of the One Ring, and he lost a fucking finger in that ordeal."

Lauren turned toward me with a smirk. "She gets to be sassy because she found my dress on her first try."

Shaking her head, Andy said, "You were looking at traditional princess-y dresses and super crazy trendy dresses—as if any of that was you—and forgetting that you're fun, cute, and sexy." Andy glanced at the shimmery aqua paint going down on my toes. Best I could tell, she was sticking with black polish. I'd never seen her in anything lighter. "You're fun, too. No poufy tulle ball gowns or cathedral trains for you, Tiel."

"I am just trying to digest the idea of getting *married* again. I can't start thinking about the wedding-industrial complex yet," I cried. "There's a million things I'm trying to figure out right now, the least of which is what I'll wear, and…*fuck*, this is overwhelming."

Lauren dumped the contents of her glass into mine. I stared at it, certain I couldn't manage that much tequila.

"You've been engaged for what? Five days? You're doing the best you can, and that's all you have to do."

"When you *are* ready, give me a call," Andy said, completely ignoring my momentary freak-out. "I'd love to look at dresses with you."

Lauren leaned toward me, and stage-whispered, "She has wedding fever."

"I do not have wedding fever," Andy said, holding out her glass for a refill. "I happen to enjoy weddings, and all the beautiful things that go into them. It's the one time that people are completely fanciful in their decision-making, and I dig that shit."

"Oh, you'll love this," Lauren said, dropping her hand on Andy's arm. "One of the teachers at my school is getting married over the summer, and the whole thing is Harry Potter-themed. I saw the mock-up of her invitations today. So cute. I didn't tell her that you'd want to steal it because brides want everything to be unique to them, but I wanted to snatch a copy for your super-secret wedding pin board."

While Lauren and Andy discussed the details of a wizarding wedding, I pushed back my panic once again. I knew I wouldn't be able to conquer any of it until I cut the strings on my up-and-down relationship with my parents. To be fair, it was mostly down, but my father made a point of calling and sending regular emails, and I counted those gestures as ups.

Even if they were loaded with passive-aggressive guilt trips.

My first instinct was to pass on the Thanksgiving invitation. I wanted to interpret it as a lukewarm peace offering, but I knew it was nothing more than an inspection. My parents wanted to get a look at my fiancé, and it didn't matter whether he was Gandhi, JJ Watt, and Bill Gates rolled into one incredible package because they'd find fault somewhere. As the polish dried on my toes and Andy continued gushing about the fun she'd have planning a Harry Potter wedding, I started wondering whether I had it all wrong.

Years of self-preservation taught me that I was better when I had some distance from them. I doubted myself less, and their dismissive comments owned less real estate in my mind. But I was beginning to believe it was time for me to go home and turn in my Disappointing Daughter card.

After Lauren, Andy, and I parted with promises to meet for lunch soon, and devised some aggressive plans to get Shannon out of the office, Sam and I grabbed a late dinner at a trendy taqueria that we loved. Though I knew he was itching to ask whether we were headed to New Jersey later this month, I didn't want to discuss it in a crowded restaurant. Our best conversations were the ones we had in bed. It wasn't about sex; it was the shelter of intimacy that we'd created, and I craved our cocoon.

"How was class today?" Sam asked.

We were tucked close together at the bar, our elbows bumping as we traded pots of guacamole, chimichurri, and tomatillo salsa. Somewhere in recent months, we adopted some new eateries and watering holes as our favored spots, and redefined our preferred activities. We still enjoyed plenty of live music, but I didn't feel as though my soul was withering if we missed a few shows anymore.

I shrugged and took a bite of my taco before responding. "Good."

He peered at me over the rim of his glasses, his eyebrow

raised and his lips twitching into a smile. "Seriously, Tiel. Turn down the enthusiasm."

I avoided Sam's eyes, instead busying myself with the guacamole.

I truly believed that I was going to grow into my new role any day. It was everything that I wanted: days spent teaching and researching music therapy at the collegiate level, and a respectable salary and benefits. It was a sensible, stable job.

But that sensible, stable job forced me to cut way back on private music sessions with my little buddies, and the pressure to get tenured was suffocating. My YouTube posts had slowed to a trickle. There were days when my violin workouts—I was deep into Bach's solo repertoire, a body of work that was so rich and transcendent that I often found myself discovering new nooks and crannies with each attempt—felt uninspired. Where I once had an endless well of research topics in mind, the pail was now coming up empty. I figured I'd get the hang of it all before the fall term ended, and if I didn't, there was always time to reboot during the spring term.

It was nothing more than an adjustment period. After many years spent in grad student mode, my brain was still trying to catch up to tenure-track professor mode. I was going to get through this, I knew it.

Sam pressed his knee into my thigh, and said, "Talk to me. Total honesty, remember?"

"It *was* a good class," I conceded. "We discussed interventional models, and I love getting into the different structures available because students at this level tend to think therapy is a never-ending prescription, which is clearly ridiculous because any treatment should succeed in *treating* and remedying the issue."

"If it's ever not a good class, you'll tell me. Right?"

"Definitely," I said. "And how was your day, darling?"

Sam cringed, and laughed as he handled the bill. "I told you about Matt's engineering episode. Aside from that special moment, I'm looking forward to this project. It's a beautiful Second Empire-style Victorian property out in Brookline. It's the perfect chunk of land for sustainable design, and now that Riley's running the entire Turlan restoration with minimal supervision, I can focus on this."

I swirled my straw around my water glass. "Why are you guys so hard on him?"

"Riley?" Sam asked, and I nodded. He frowned, scratched his chin, and stared at the bottles of tequila lined up on the bar. "We're not *that* hard on him."

"Maybe you don't notice it," I said. "But it's no fun being the fuck-up, and I'm speaking from experience."

"We don't..." His voice trailed off and he frowned again, deeper this time.

"Think about it," I said, running my hand over his shoulders. "I know that busting each other's balls is in your DNA and it's all hate-love with you guys, but Riley gets it the most."

Sam tapped his credit card on the bar for a few seconds before nodding and replacing it in his wallet. "Do you think he's..."

"Hurt? Emotionally damaged? Suffering from low self-esteem?" I asked. "No. None of the above. He doesn't let much bother him—at least I don't think so—and he's really laid back. But he doesn't have to reprise the role of black sheep every day, either."

"Good," Sam murmured. "Emotionally damaged is my shtick. There's no room for him in this corner."

"Your humor is remarkably dark," I said. "Now take me home. I need some snuggletime."

True to form, Riley was sprawled on the sofa with his hand in his boxers when we returned to the firehouse. He was flipping back and forth between several games, and only grunted when we told him we were turning in for the evening.

Once inside the somewhat enclosed second-floor space that functioned as our bedroom and open-air closets, Sam asked, "Did you notice?"

I was busy taking off my beaded bracelets and bib necklace. "Notice what?"

"Back there. Just now. I was going to ask Riley if he was trying to find his dick but I *didn't*. I listened to you."

Turning around as I removed my rose quartz earrings, I said, "That's real progress, Sam."

I withheld a chuckle until the bathroom door closed behind him. After changing out of my dress and into a t-shirt, I heard him rustling in his bedside drawers. He was setting out the equipment to replace his blood glucose monitor's infusion set. The fact that he was standing there shirtless, with the insulin ports on either side of his belly button exposed, said everything about the distance we'd crossed together.

"Hey," he said, beckoning me closer. He folded me into his arms when I approached, and I laid my head on his chest. "I love you. Also noteworthy: your tits look amazing in this shirt."

His hands moved down my back to squeeze my backside as I laughed. "I love you, too," I said. "And…we need to talk."

His chin bobbed against my head. "I know. Let me switch this out, and then we'll get comfortable."

I retreated to the bathroom and gave Sam some privacy to handle his device. He'd been increasingly open about his glucose monitoring, but just as I didn't want him watching while I bleached the fuzz on my upper lip, he preferred some space.

Once my teeth were brushed and makeup scrubbed off, I joined Sam under the covers. His glasses were perched on the bedside table and his hair was a little wild, and I was angry that I'd spent entire days doubting whether I was enough for this man.

"Get over here," Sam said, his arms spread wide. "And lose the shirt."

"What happened to my tits looking amazing in this shirt?" I crawled toward him. "Besides, I'm not letting you have any boob action until we discuss some stuff."

He drew the blankets over us and tugged me closer. This was my favorite spot in the world, right here with his body warm against mine. I could surrender everything to Sam, and I'd always feel safe and strong and cherished.

"'Letting you'? It's really precious when you try to take the lead," he said.

His lips dropped to my neck, and *oh yes,* my body was more interested in this than any of the knots in my mind. I shivered, and wrapped my hand around his forearm.

"Are you trying to distract me?" I asked.

"Nope," he said. The word vibrated against my neck, and it rippled through my body.

I was on the verge of annoyed, but then his fingertips

started working my back and shoulders, and I realized where this was going. He was softening me up. He knew I was tense, and he was helping me get the words out.

If this was what our forever was going to feel like—ass grabbing and diabetes management, understanding each other beyond words and going to bed before eleven o'clock simply because we liked holding each other—there was no reason for my panic. Relieved tears filled my eyes, and I burrowed further into his arms.

I knew how to love Sam. He was mine, and I didn't need any vintage inadequacy getting in the way.

"I have some conditions," I said. I traced the fishhook tattoo on Sam's upper arm. "But I think...I think we should visit my family in New Jersey for the holiday."

"Tell me more," Sam said, his words muffled as he spoke into my hair. "Walk me through this. I want to hear what you're thinking, and your conditions."

"Remember when I went home for Christmas last year?"

"Vividly," Sam said.

"Then you remember how I wanted to leave because it was awful," I said, and he nodded. "And I told you the next time I was going to Jersey, you were coming with me."

"I admire your follow-through here, but I'm hoping you have another reason lined up," he said.

"I always hated helping out at my family's restaurant. It was a chore that I dreaded, and to me, it was a punishment. A long, boring loop of chopping vegetables, stacking plates, filling baskets of pita bread." I stared at the fishhook and exhaled. "I was the only one who felt that way. My sister, my cousins, they loved being at the restaurant. They knew they belonged there, but it wasn't like that for me."

Sam didn't say anything while I paused, but his hands continued rubbing and pressing along my spine.

"There were a lot of events at the restaurant. Parties, celebrations, feasts. Sometimes I performed traditional Greek songs. Everyone loved it, and playing in front of crowds from such a young age is probably why I never dealt with stage fright. See? There's the silver lining. Remind me of that later."

"Done," Sam said.

"I played at an event one night, and it was so great. I performed well, the music sounded good, the people enjoyed it…I was floating ten feet off the ground. It was one of the first moments when I felt like I belonged."

My finger brushed the tattoo above Sam's heart, the new sunburst one with my name woven into the shape.

"You know when you're young, and you overhear adults talking about things you don't understand? I was always listening to my family while I worked, and I never thought much about it. But that night, I remember walking down the hallway to the back office after I performed, and stopping before I got to the door. My mom was crying, and telling my aunt that she didn't understand why I was such a difficult kid. Why was I hyperactive? Why did I hate Greek school and church groups? Why couldn't I like the same things as my cousins? Why did I always have to be different? Why couldn't I be more like Agapi? Why was I only willing to come to the restaurant if it was to play that screechy violin?"

Sam held me tighter, and I clung to him as if I was warding against a slide into another time and place. "It's because you can't be anyone else. There's no forcing you into a mold. You're rare and wild, Sunshine."

"I didn't go in there. I went out into the alley and played The Who's 'Tommy' album until it was time to go home. And then…I overheard the same conversation last Christmas. Like nothing had changed, in all these years."

I touched the sunburst as I blinked away tears. I wasn't crying over this; me and my big girl panties were beyond this bullshit. But I couldn't dip my toes into wedding planning waters until I'd conquered something—*fucking anything*—with my family. Ultimately, this visit to New Jersey was going to determine whether my family had a place in my life. I was holding out hope that this would be the moment when they looked at me with new eyes, and accepted that, while my choices were different, I was worthy.

"Sometimes I walk away from things I don't want to deal with. I do my own thing, I avoid, I hope it gets better while I'm not paying attention. But…I've spent every day this week worried that you were going to realize I wasn't enough for you, and—"

"Tiel," he interrupted, his tone sharp. "Do *not* finish that sentence."

I shifted to meet his eyes, and when I did, I found every shade of anger and hurt on his face. "I can't walk away anymore."

Sam's lips were pressed together in a tight grimace and his eyes were cast down. "We need to go back to the part about you feeling like you're anything less than my everything," he said. "I won't let you talk about yourself, or us, that way. Let me be your safe space, Tiel."

"You are my safe space, Sam," I said. "You always have been. But this isn't about me. I think I understand that now, and I'm trying to remind myself of that, but I have to deal with it this time. I can't walk away."

"If you're sure you want to do this, believe me when I say that I'm not letting anyone hurt you," he said. "I'm not going to stand for any of that shit, Tiel. If we're doing this, we're only doing as much as you're comfortable with. And we're not staying at your parents' house. I need to be able to rip your panties off and spank you without concern for who might be listening."

"I was hoping you'd say that."

Sam sat up and gestured to my neon pink polka-dotted panties. "Allow me to demonstrate."

A couple of months ago, Shannon and Lauren threw down over the topic of panty-ripping. Shannon argued that underwear weren't made of paper, and they didn't tear as easily as some liked to believe. Lauren insisted that Matt had been known to rip a pair or two, and when the right fabric was in the right hands, the task wasn't insurmountable.

I didn't wade into that argument, but not because I didn't have strong feelings about it. No, my greater concern was suffering a bout of word vomit and accidentally mentioning that I'd been sitting at brunch bare-assed because Sam tore my last clean pair off me that morning.

Much like the ones he tore off just now.

"Are you going to be quiet?" he asked, my shredded panties hanging off his finger and the gleam in his eye telling me that every answer was the right one.

*Three*

TIEL

*November*

**I HAD** to tell Sam we weren't pregnant this month, and that was difficult for a few reasons.

To start, I hated talking about my period. With anyone. Ever. I didn't have major issues associated with menstruation or anything, but it wasn't something we discussed openly in my home when I was growing up. Ladies were supposed to keep those things to themselves.

Second, Sam was disappointed. He allowed it to flicker over his expression for a quick moment, but it was there.

Finally, and perhaps most importantly, we were operating under the assumption that this was going to be easy. While this was only our third month of trying, our approach to *trying* was the definition of weaksauce. It was limited to no condoms, lots of sex, and hoping it all worked out well.

There was never a time in the history of Sam and Tiel that things simply *worked out well*.

We needed strategy, we needed timing, and we needed to stop with "Sunshine, I just want to come all over your tits right now."

That was how I ended up sifting through bulk bins at an herb and spice market in Somerville when I was supposed to be harassing Shannon. My portion of today's plan involved me stopping by her apartment, and cajoling her into joining us for lunch. She could ignore calls and texts, but she couldn't ignore a Saturday morning pop-in.

Shannon and I weren't close, and I wanted to change that. Our relationship was rocky from the start, and plenty of that was my fault. I didn't want to put Sam in the position of having to choose me over his siblings, and if that meant I was inviting her along for holiday weekends when she was sad and lonely, or conspiring to get her mimosa-drunk on the weekend, I was doing it.

But first, I was getting my hands on some red clover and racking my brain for the rest of my great-grandmother's special fertility tea recipe. When the kettle was on the stove and those dried flowers were in the strainer, everyone knew it was time to start knitting baby blankets because that tea never failed.

The recipe was the one gift my great-grandmother gave at bridal showers. Sometimes there was a loaf of scratch-made olive bread with the tea recipe, but only if she *really* liked you.

Without that recipe and with my luck, I'd flub the ingredients or ratios, and end up with hair on my chest or an accidental cure for indigestion. But that wasn't going to hold me back. Nope, I was full steam ahead with my smelly tea and a new app on my phone to track the comings-and-goings in my lady regions.

Once I'd navigated my way to Shannon's neighborhood, it took another twenty minutes to find a parking spot, and I was far behind schedule. Things didn't get much better. There was the odd moment of finding a very wet, very large, very tattooed, and very nearly naked man behind Shannon's door—he looked like a mighty fine way to recover from a breakup—and then the splendor of babbling that information to Andy and Lauren before discovering that Shannon wished to keep it private.

How I was supposed to know that Tattooed-and-Toweled was meant to be a secret was beyond me. Through it all, I pissed off my future sister-in-law *again*, guzzled four too many mimosas, managed to eat none of my lunch, and had to call in a favor to get my drunk ass home.

I was leaning beside a trough of butternut squash, alternately eyeing the phallic shape and laughing at my own quips when I spotted him near the main entrance.

"Hey," Riley said as I approached. My head was still swimming with light, fizzy bubbles, and I was working damn hard to keep from wobbling.

"Hi," I said, "and thank you for coming so quickly."

"Yeah, no problem. I was at the office, so I was close," he said. His hand landed on my shoulder, steadying me, and he leveled me with a skeptical look. "Everything okay?"

I nodded, and the sensation in my head was slow, reminiscent of shaking an Etch A Sketch. "I can't keep up with them," I confessed. "I don't know how those women can drink like that, and on a Saturday afternoon, no less. It's like they run on liquor and nonfat yogurt, and Sephora samples."

"Don't forget about the cupcakes." Riley tightened his grip on my shoulder as he laughed. "Where are you parked, Punky Brewster?"

I led the way, wobbling and nearly wiping out on a cracked segment of the sidewalk, and handed over the keys to Sam's Range Rover when it came into sight. Without a word, Riley turned the ignition and merged into the afternoon traffic.

"You're not going to ask?" I studied him while we were stopped at a light near Faneuil Hall. "About me texting you in the middle of the day to drive me home, and not calling Sam instead? I'm sure I dragged you away from something fun."

"At the *office*?" Riley shook his head. "Nope."

"I've had a lot of champagne, and think I'm gonna tell you anyway."

He tugged at the knotted man-bun sitting loose at the nape of his neck. "I don't fuckin' understand what it is about chicks and brunch."

"Sam's in his workshop, which means he's not going to hear his phone over the saws, and he's been all fired up about getting some table finished." Slouching deeper into the seat, I sighed. "I still can't figure out what to say around your sister. I'm always going on about the wrong things, or saying too much or not enough, or it comes out all wrong. Even when I try to help, I screw up."

I wanted to find my groove with these women. It didn't escape my notice that I'd already flamed out of one family, and I didn't want that track record following me here. But befriending adult women on the basis of our shared love for the Walsh brothers was an oversimplification of the matter. The presumption that all significant others and sisters-in-law would automatically become besties only made sense if these boys were in the market for the exact same woman, and I could attest they weren't.

Liking each other and becoming good friends wasn't merely a dress that you put on. No, it had to look right, feel right, *fit*.

And right now, despite all my best efforts, I didn't fit. At least not with Shannon.

"She'll get over it," he said. He rested his elbow on the center console and gestured toward me as we crossed the Congress Street Bridge. "Contrary to popular belief, she doesn't hold grudges. She gives everyone seven or eight second chances."

"Hmm," I murmured. "I don't think I qualify for that package."

"You do." Riley clicked the automatic door opener and drove into the old fire truck bay. "Hell, I think I'm on second chance number twenty-nine. Don't sweat it." He pointed at the street, and said, "I'm going to get some work done at Turlan. It's easier when there isn't as much noise, or people. There are all these old medallions to fix, and I can't believe anyone accepts the quality I'm getting from Sam's plaster craftsman. It's horrendous. I'd rather do it all by hand, myself, than let that shit fly, and…yeah. Don't worry about me for dinner or anything."

"Thanks for the save," I called as he backed out.

"No sweat," he said. "You've saved my ass plenty of times. And remember: there's no bite in Shannon's bark."

I wasn't sure that theory extended beyond Shannon's siblings, but Riley was already cruising down the street, and the argument dissolved on my tongue.

I stumbled inside and then into Sam's workshop, and

found him running boards through the circular saw. He was dressed in a black tank top and the old pair of low-slung jeans he always wore when he was woodworking. And the battered gloves. Jesus, there was something about jeans, a tank top, and work gloves that screamed "Come a little closer so I can defile you."

That look turned my thoughts into dark, sticky molasses.

There had been times when I'd tried to look at him in this gear without turning into a stuttering pile of hormones, but it always ended with me climbing him like a tree.

I boosted myself up on the edge of the work table and watched his arms and shoulders flexing against the saw's vibrations. He hadn't lost any of that lumberjacked strength.

*Slow, slow molasses.*

When he finished, he shifted the safety glasses to the top of his head and shoved his gloves in his back pocket. "Why are you sitting on my table and looking guilty?" he asked.

"I'm having some very dirty thoughts about you right now, and I got drunk at lunch and I broke Shannon," I blurted.

Sam braced his hands on either side of me and leaned forward. "Tell me all your dirty thoughts, drunk girl."

*Oh, hell. Those arms.*

I was raking my gaze over them like they were fresh meat.

"I broke Shannon," I repeated, but instead of retreating, Sam moved farther into my space. His lips coasted over my neck and across my chest. He pulled my sweater down, exposing the swell of my breasts. He buried his face there, kissing, licking, sucking.

"Was this one of your dirty thoughts?" he asked.

There were going to be marks. Little red spots where his teeth closed around my tender flesh with the right amount of pressure to leave memories tomorrow, but not enough to break the skin. They felt like everything, all at once, and I loved it.

"I have to confess my sins," I said, gasping as Sam's tongue found my nipple. "Lunch was really bad. I *broke* Shannon. I said all the wrong things and then Riley had to pick me up, and now he's off fixing plaster because it's quiet."

Sam gazed up at me from between my breasts, his eyebrow arched. "Is Shannon in immediate danger?"

"Unlikely," I said, thinking back to Tattooed-and-Toweled in her apartment, and his fierce, possessive stare.

"Outstanding," he said as he hauled me off the table. "I'm gonna take advantage of you now, drunk girl. Let's go talk about your dirty thoughts."

Sam marched me into our bedroom, one hand locked on my breast, the other unlatching my belt. His mouth was on my neck, and I could feel him hard against my backside.

"You look like you could do terrible things to me, and then smile about it."

"Oh, I really could," he said, his hand sliding into my jeans. "You need to be spanked."

"Yes," I moaned, melting into him.

He cupped me over my panties, rhythmically squeezing and releasing until I was aching. "It wasn't a question."

There it was: the subtle shift in our power dynamic. Gone was Fiancé Sam, the one who shared all the household chores with me, the one who was exceedingly sweet and respectful as a matter of fact. In his place was Bedroom

Sam, the one who was known to rip off my underwear and fashion it into a gag, or tease me until I was *crying* with need, or leave discernible handprints on my ass.

I loved Bedroom Sam, and I loved the people he let us be here. He understood me and everything I needed, even when I didn't understand it. There was something gorgeously liberating about gaining freedom from my own thoughts, and I merrily surrendered to him every time he demanded it and not only because it was good for me—it was fan-fucking-tastic—but it was good for him, too. It shuttered his smooth, charming façade and funneled it into a flavor of loosely chained aggression that looked better on him than any low-slung jeans or three-piece suit in existence.

His grip tightened on me for a long moment, and when it relaxed, the ache between my legs was now a drum-beating throb. "You need someone to take care of this pretty little pussy, don't you? Someone to make it feel better?"

"*Yesssss*," I said. Then I remembered. "Wait, no, I still have my period. It's just about over, but—"

"Don't care," Sam murmured against my neck. "Now take my clothes off."

Turning in his arms, I yanked the tank top over his head and drank in the sight of him. The jeans accentuated the deep grooves chiseled into his belly, the angular lines directing all attention between his legs.

"Mmmm, it's like you're not even real," I sighed, running my fingers down his chest and abs. "I'm so lucky. Have I told you that? I look at you, and all I can think is, *boom*. My panties just melted. Then I think, let me lick that boy's cock."

His head tipped back as his eyes drifted shut with a

laugh, and I watched the rise and fall of his chest as he blew out a breath, my fingers mapping the movement in wonder. *I get to keep you*, I thought, and pressure swelled in my chest as I realized, for the millionth time, that this man belonged to me. He was going to be my husband, the father of my babies, the one I grew old and most likely senile with, the one meant all for me.

"But you're not allowed to come in my mouth," I said, my words thick and slow. "Or on my tits. Nope. We're done with that, and will you help me brew some tea later?"

"I'm going to count to five," Sam said, holding up his hand. "And when I'm finished, I want you naked and kneeling."

I nodded toward the bathroom. "Give me a minute first, but..." I bit my lower lip and lifted my eyebrows. "Maybe you could finish getting undressed and stroke your cock until I get back? Or, if you wanted to keep doing it, I wouldn't mind watching."

"You have one minute," Sam said, biting out each word. "And when that minute is over, I expect to see you on your knees with my cock in your mouth, and you will not be calling the plays anymore, sweetheart."

Hungry to comply, I stripped out of my clothes and got myself ready. When I returned to the bedroom, Sam was standing beside the bed, the blankets turned down, his jeans open and his hand wrapped around his shaft.

Rooted in place, I watched as his forearm rippled with each stroke.

"Get over here," he barked, gesturing to the space between his legs as he sat on the bed. I went, dropping to my knees and waiting until his hand fisted in my hair. It was then, and not a second sooner, that he wanted my mouth.

I took him in, savoring the weight of him on my tongue. But I wasn't allowed to savor long. Sam released a heavy, impatient growl as his hips started jerking forward, and his grip tightened around my hair. His free hand moved from my shoulder up my neck, his fingers grazing my cheek with all the tenderness his bucking hips lacked, and this was how I loved him most. Wild and rough, and never more than a blink away from flat-out adoration.

He rocked into my mouth with a punishing pace, and his body became taut and restless under my palms, his words turned more impatient, more filthy. There was nothing he wouldn't say when I was here, and I craved every growl and command like it was a favorite old song, one I knew by heart and that had my body swaying with the beat at the opening chords.

My fingertips moved over his muscular thighs and between his legs, back, *back*, stroking and teasing, and wringing another snap of pleasure from him. With a gasp, he released my hair and slowed his thrusts until he was lazily jabbing into my mouth. He was backing away from the brink.

"Oh, my pervy girl," he growled. "What am I going to do with you?"

I smiled up at him, leaning into the hand cradling my face, and offered a shrug packed with as much coquettishness as I could gather with a dick in my mouth. He responded in kind with a sharp jab into my mouth before pulling all the way out.

He liked to force me, just a bit and only when I liked it, too, and he stuttered out an obscene string of curse-laced groans when my lips stiffened, offering the thick head of his cock some resistance as he pushed into me.

"If you don't want me coming in your mouth, your ass needs to get on that bed and your legs need to be spread for me because I'm not interested in waiting." His fingers stroked over my hair, slow and gentle, as if he was trying to remind me that his sweetness was lurking in the background while his greediness took charge. "I love you," Sam whispered.

"The sheets," I said. "Let me put down a towel, or—"

"Don't care."

And with that, he pulled me onto the bed, wrenched my legs open, and sank inside me. The only response I could manage was a slurred, sloppy amalgam of incomplete words.

"What was that?" Sam asked, and the glint in his voice told me that he was fully aware of his cock's brain-scrambling powers.

The light, wiry hairs on his chest scraped over my breasts, taunting my nipples with not enough friction while he drove into me, his fingers digging into my thighs as he pinned my legs wide. His skin was hot to the touch, and his hold was nearly painful, but that bite of pain only accentuated the deep, drugging pleasure of his cock as it pounded into me. He shifted up on his knees, drew my legs back toward the mattress, and gazed at where we were joined.

This angle did *terrible* things to me. It always felt like a new depth, a territory previously uncharted, and the one word I could only ever manage to broadcast my praise was Sam's name, over and over again.

And I knew it was the same for him, too. The sweat beading on his forehead and sharp, determined set of his jaw told me he was working hard to prolong the moment, but his increasingly frenzied hums and groans told me it wasn't working.

Sam's breathing faltered, coming out in a choked huff before he was bringing his eyes up my body to meet mine. "*Get there*, Tiel," he said.

"I can't— I can't—"

"Yes, you can."

I was gasping, hiccupping when Sam's hand slid down the back of my thigh to caress my ass before winding up to deliver rapid-fire blows.

"I'm not waiting for you, drunk girl," he snarled.

That was a lie, but my orgasm didn't understand that— never did—and it uncoiled, slow like a summer sunset, then too fast and weighty for me to do anything but cry out as it engulfed me. I stayed lost in that fog as Sam cornered his own release and eventually dropped to the mattress.

"That was incredible. Really fucking incredible," he said. He reached out, blindly groping beside him before his hand connected with my belly. "Yeah?"

I hummed in agreement.

"I want to know exactly what you were drinking because I'm buying several cases of it tonight."

Covering my face with my hands, I laughed. "Oh no. I'm on the No-More-Mimosas plan."

"Not sure I can support that initiative," Sam said, his fingertips drawing circles between my belly button and bikini line. "It worked out favorably for me."

"If you want to get me drunk and silly, I'm willing to oblige you here, at home. Not at lunch with the girls. I really did fuck things up with Shannon," I said.

"My dick is still wet," Sam said, his face buried in the

pillow as he groaned. "I don't want to talk about my sister right now. I just want to hold you for a little while and maybe rub your tits, and then, later, *much later*, we can sort out Shannon's issues."

"I should go clean up first," I said, sitting up and surveying the linens. They seemed fine, and that was a relief.

"We'll buy new sheets," Sam yelled into the pillow before flopping over to pull me down to the mattress. "Just cuddle me, woman."

My arms banded around his shoulders, he nestled his head between my breasts—the one spot he adored more than anywhere else on earth—and we stayed there, quietly breathless and unwilling to stop touching.

There were so many things that I loved about Sam, and our relationship, but they always seemed to crystallize when we were skin to skin and bathed in post-orgasmic bliss. Everything that existed around us, before us, beyond us, faded. It was in these moments that he wasn't merely a good, caring man who also happened to be a fucking beast in bed, but he was *my* man.

"All right, that's long enough," he said eventually. He rolled over and sat up, stretching his arms over his head. "Next round in the shower?"

*Four*

SAM

*November*

THE DRIVE to New Jersey was long and uneventful, save for the tension radiating off Tiel. She chattered all the way through Massachusetts and Connecticut, barely pausing from sharing the gory details of the college's latest scandal to take a breath. It seemed a professor was caught in a *delicate* situation with one of his students. Since that story broke, Tiel and the rest of the college personnel were required to attend several hours of refresher trainings on sexual harassment, fraternization, and ethics policies.

There was no clean opening to press on whether working in higher education was bringing her the fulfillment and purpose she craved. It wasn't, but I couldn't force her into that realization. And maybe this wasn't the weekend for all the realizations to detonate at once.

Lingering over a late lunch outside New York City, Tiel ranked her top Broadway shows (*Rent, Avenue Q, The Book of Mormon, Les Misérables, The Phantom of the Opera, Wicked, Hedwig and the Angry Inch,* and *The Lion King;* she was obsessed with the soundtrack but was withholding full judgment on *Hamilton* until we saw the show). In her mind, musical theater was the *only* theater.

We agreed we were due for a trip to Manhattan, and that set her off on a tangent about her favorite New York hole-in-the-wall music venues. She didn't talk about her Juilliard years often, and I liked hearing her account of these events without the shadow of her ex-husband looming large. I hated the guy for the way he threw Tiel away when he was done with her, but based on what I knew of her family, it was clear he wasn't the only one.

When we crossed into New Jersey, Tiel's stories slowed, and she turned her attention to commenting on Spotify playlists. They all got the Goldilocks treatment—too long, too short, too boring, too random—but I loved her noise. She viewed the world through a lens that fascinated and confused me, and I was crazy for it. I wanted to know everything, all of her.

After we passed Newark, she stopped talking altogether. She twisted her fingers in her necklaces as she stared out the window, and she was changing before my eyes.

Her near-constant tapping, swaying, and humming along with the music shifted to erratic finger-drumming. The bright, easy smile that was never far from her face transformed into a hard line, and her warmth dimmed by degrees.

Hours separated us from visiting Tiel's parents tomorrow, and I was hoping the hotel I'd chosen had an above-average selection of adult entertainment. I wasn't about to let this anxiety claim her, not when I could throw her legs over my shoulders and fuck the stress right out of her while she watched some high-quality girl-on-girl.

And it wasn't like that would be a hardship for me to endure, either.

* * *

**TIEL'S MOTHER** held the wine bottle at an arm's length and peered at the label as if it was a foreign object.

"That's so...nice," she murmured before glancing up at us. "Is this popular in Boston?"

"Yes, Mom, it's a very cosmopolitan wine," Tiel said dryly, "but you're a fan of red wine. I think you'll like this."

"Well, I don't drink nearly as much as you do," she said, her forced smile wavering into a grimace. "We'll save it for a special occasion."

Two things were noteworthy.

One, Mrs. Desai could throw shade at a sunflower. Her expression upon opening the door was a mixture of contempt and grudging acceptance, as if she'd lost a bet on whether we'd show up, and it hadn't gotten any better.

Two, we'd been clustered in the doorway for fifteen fucking uncomfortable minutes. There was a stiff embrace between Tiel and her mother followed by a handshake for me, and then long, silent moments where she stared at us with a smile so fake it belonged on a Botox ad. It was unclear whether we'd be invited in past the foyer.

In the absence of anything else to discuss, Tiel drew her mother's attention to the gift basket I was still clutching.

"Yeah, maybe we could put this down," Tiel said, glancing at the basket.

She was wearing a dark green wrap dress with a hot

pink quatrefoil print from a legendary designer, one that I'd insisted on purchasing when she helped me pick out new Oxford shirts and ties last month. It did amazing things for her body, and she knew it, too. She wasn't comfortable with me spending money on her—that needed to change *real* soon—but she liked to call this her power dress. It was the one that made her feel every ounce of the goddess she was, and I knew she was wearing it because she required that boost today.

But based on Mrs. Desai's expression, Tiel might as well have been wearing a potato sack.

I didn't understand how anyone could look at her without being bowled over by her untamed, unabashed beauty. Sure, she was wearing four amber necklaces and silver mermaid earrings, but that was Tiel and she made it look damn good.

"Oh, hello! Tiel!" A barrel-chested man came around the corner, a dish towel draped over his shoulder, and held his arms out. He brought Tiel in for a firm hug, and then extended his hand to me. "You must be Sam."

We shook, and he insisted that I call him Vikram, and things didn't seem too bad.

Then, a gaggle of women descended upon us. They all bore a striking resemblance to each other and spoke with New Jersey accents thick enough to resemble a foreign tongue. One plucked the basket from my hold, another took Tiel by the hand and pulled her into the living room, and another deposited an infant in my arms.

Despite having an urgent desire to start a family with Tiel, I couldn't remember the last time I'd held a baby. It was like having a soft-yet-solid sack of wiggling sugar in my arms, and that sack of sugar had no problem curling her chubby fingers around my linen pocket square and tugging it free.

"Do you have a name?" I asked. She responded by rapping her socked feet on my arm.

"That's Angelina," Vikram said from behind me. "She's Demitria's youngest. She'll be six months next week." He gestured to the women surrounding Tiel, but I couldn't tell them apart.

"Hi, Angelina," I said. "You're a cutie."

Her face broke into a wide smile, and her legs never ceased kicking. She chomped on my pocket square, and something inside me stirred. I didn't even know this kid and I was melting for her.

"You're just a precious little package, aren't you, Angelina?" I asked her. She giggled around the pocket square, her bright eyes twinkling.

Behind me, Tiel's parents were carrying on a conversation in what I could only assume was Greek. The words were hushed but the tone was tense.

"Oh, no. She'll ruin that," Mrs. Desai said. She stepped closer and gestured toward Angelina and the pocket square she was slobbering all over.

I shook my head, unconcerned. "I don't mind," I said. "She can keep it."

Mrs. Desai—she hadn't invited me to call her Ilonna yet—loosened the cloth from the baby's hold. After scraping her gaze over my blue Helmut Lang suit, she frowned. "Tiel's never mentioned you before this...announcement. Have you been seeing each other long?"

There wasn't a right answer here. If I admitted we'd been together for more than a year, Tiel was getting hammered for withholding information. If I shaved some time off that figure, Tiel was getting hammered for being impetuous.

"Long enough to know she's the only one for me," I said.

I found myself rocking from side to side, and patting the baby's diapered bottom. I couldn't stop looking at this giggly, drooly, tiny human, and it felt…natural.

For the second time this afternoon, Mrs. Desai forced an uncomfortable smile and said, "That's so…nice." She reached for Angelina. "I'll take her now."

Without an infant to dominate my attention, I was suddenly aware of the noise around me. The women who dragged Tiel into the living room were talking, all at once.

"Your mother said you were engaged, but I didn't believe her."

"I thought you were moving home to help your sister with the baby."

"You're *engaged*? Since when?"

"Someone get a corkscrew. I'm drinkin' this wine, it looks fancy."

"Oh my God, let me see your ring!"

"Is that him? You're engaged to *him*? He's a piece of somethin' nice."

"Your mother said you're teaching kindergarten but also waitressing to make ends meet. Does your fiancé approve of that? When I got engaged, Stav *insisted* that I stay home."

"That's just like *Pretty Woman*! I love that movie so much."

"*Pretty Woman* was a hooker. Waitressing is horrendous, but it's not hooking unless you're waitressing in a sex club."

"Hold up. Did you meet him at a sex club? I read a book about a sex club, I swear to you, I thought it was going to be all smut but they fell in love and I cried. It was an ugly, ugly cry. I couldn't help it."

"Why is it pink? It's not supposed to be pink. Real diamonds are *not* pink. I know my four Cs."

"I don't know how you do it. I couldn't get married at your age. I wouldn't even want to be pregnant at your age."

"If Costas gave me a pink diamond, I'd hand it back and say, try again, sir."

"Are you on prenatal vitamins? Do it, your hair and nails will thank me. And it's good for the baby, too."

"You're gonna need hair extensions. This is not bride hair."

"He looks like a lawyer. Are you a lawyer? A banker? What d'you do, honey?"

"Jennifer Lopez had a pink diamond when she was engaged to Ben Affleck."

"Is that his Range Rover outside? That's special."

"And that marriage did *not* occur. Look at the bullet she dodged."

"Where is that corkscrew? It's two o'clock on a *holiday* and I don't have a glass of wine. This is why I like screw caps."

"You need a shellac manicure. Tell your boyfriend to get you one, it looks like he can afford it."

"You know who he looks like? That one that I like from that show, you know which one."

"Oh, yeah, I like that one, too. But I think he's married. Or gay. Or gay married."

"What kind of cut is this? It's not princess and it's not brilliant."

"Maybe it was an accident. It's supposed to be one cut or another, not round *and* square."

"We don't say gay married anymore. It's just married. It's not politically correct."

"Who can keep up with politically correct? My God, it's a nightmare."

"Are those real Tory Burch flats or the knockoffs?"

"Oh my God, I love your dress. Can I try it on? My boobs are obviously bigger but that's not a problem. I like them to be out there and all *hello*!"

"You should see my Louis Vuitton knockoff. It's amazing. You'd never know."

Now, with voices spinning around Tiel like an estrogen-fueled tornado, I understood why she struggled with big, noisy families. Hell, I was ready for a stiff drink and a quiet corner, and I wasn't the one stuck in the eye of the storm.

"Irene, Demitria, Nicki, Nikki, Penny, Agapi," Vikram called. "Your mothers need your help in the kitchen."

The women continued talking, lapsing into intermittent Greek as they filed out, and Tiel followed. Pulling her close to me when she passed, I said, "Where are you going?"

"Kitchen," she whispered. She leaned her head against my chest and her shoulders dropped. "They're going to keep speculating on whether my shoes are authentic and diamonds can be pink, and at least one of them is going to have something to say about you being a piece of something nice. They're also going to talk about me being a spoiled brat if I don't help, so…"

"My goal in life is to spoil you, so wear it well." I kissed her temple and inhaled her sweet scent. "You got this, Sunshine."

"Go find another baby to hold. There are at least four or five of them crawling around," she said, laughing. "It was precious. My ovaries exploded."

I dipped my head to catch her eyes. "Do I want your ovaries to explode?"

"Uh, yeah, you do," she said. "Much more of that and I'm going to be pregnant before we walk out of here."

***

"NOW, SAM," one of Tiel's cousins—or maybe her sister? they really *did* look alike—said. "What do you do?"

We were seated at a long, makeshift table, surrounded by two dozen of Tiel's family members. "I'm an architect," I said, accepting a plate loaded with lamb, vegetables, and rice from Tiel.

She offered a quick nod, and I knew she'd weeded out anything that would trigger my food allergies.

*This* was what it meant to be spoiled. I fucking loved this girl.

"Really?" the sister-cousin asked. "Like, construction? No offense, but I know construction and you don't look like construction to me."

There was an insult hiding in there, but I wasn't about to go find it.

"Sam designs multimillion dollar homes and supervises the construction, Agapi," Tiel said. Ah. That *was* her sister. "One of his houses was featured in *Vogue* last month."

To be fair, it was the internet start-up billionaire whose home I restored that was featured in *Vogue* in last month. The accompanying photo shoot took place at the Manchester-by-the-Sea home, and there was a brief reference to our restoration of the property.

But I knew what Tiel was doing. I liked seeing her step up to the plate for me.

Agapi nodded, taking this in, and pointed at Tiel with her glass. "What are you doing now? I know you said you had *things going on* and that was why you *didn't want to* mind Anatola while I was at the restaurant, so...did you find work? Or are you just focused on wedding planning now?"

Okay, my turn. This bitch was going down.

"Tiel has quite a bit *going on*. She's one of the top music therapy professors in Boston," I said, "and her research has been used as the gold standard in early intervention for children on the autism spectrum. There aren't enough hours in the day for all the private therapy and consulting requests she gets."

She caught my eye, and the corner of her lips tipped up into a small, shy smile.

"I thought you were a kindergarten teacher," one of her cousins said. She was either Nicola or Nicolina, also known as Nicki or Nikki, and that wasn't confusing at all. She turned to Mrs. Desai. "Where did I hear that?"

Mrs. Desai pressed her palms together as she lifted her shoulders. "We never hear from you," she said to Tiel. "And you're always between jobs. How can we possibly keep up with your life?"

Vikram was seated at the far end of the table, and if he was listening to this bullshit, it didn't show. In the few hours that we'd been here, it was clear that was his standard operating procedure. He was pleased to see Tiel and showed a reasonable amount of hospitality toward me, but either didn't notice or didn't care about the quips, barbs, and thorny comments lobbed in her direction.

My patience for that shit was thinning.

I was ready to throw down for my girl, and it didn't

matter to me whether it got me tossed out on my ass because I already knew this shindig wasn't ending with a group hug. Call it cynicism, call it pessimism, call it whatever the fuck you wanted. Every horseman of the dysfunctional family apocalypse was accounted for, and Tiel's mother, the queen shit-stirrer, was itching to unleash them.

"There's so much demand for Tiel's music therapy expertise that she's often pulled in many directions," I said. "She's sought-after in her field."

That explanation didn't work for Mrs. Desai. She shook her head and scowled at her plate. "Music therapy," she repeated. "Is that like physical therapy?"

"They're similar," Tiel said. She was busy chasing food around her plate, but I hadn't seen her take a bite yet. "Like physical therapy, it is often used as a complement to medical and educational interventions, although music therapy is expressive in nature and physical therapy is not. My work usually integrates the Nordoff-Robbins approach to accommodate children across all levels of functionality."

The table, including the two folding tables extending this gathering across the hall and into the living room, fell silent.

"That sounds like some new age shit," Agapi's husband, Tony, said. He was the butcher, and from my brief conversation with him, I determined that he enjoyed discussing two topics: meat and the Philadelphia Eagles. That didn't leave us with much to talk about.

"We're in my mother's house, watch your language," Agapi hissed. She turned back to Tiel. "Why would someone need music therapy? Like, what does that do? What's the point?"

"Whatever the point needs to be," Tiel said. "Some kids

need to work on anxiety. Others need help learning how to stabilize their moods or increase their tolerance for frustration. Some are non-verbal and others don't speak much, and they need to develop tools for self-expression. There's no one prescription; it's whatever they need."

"I'm with Tony. That's some hippie-dippie-fruity-crunchy business," yet another cousin, Penny, said. "It's like the people who believe in crystals and chakras. If you put a rock on my body, it's not going to do anything. How could it?"

"People pay for this?" Nicolina-or-Nicola asked. "Wouldn't listening to the radio do the same thing, but free?"

"It's a little more complex than that," I said. "And Tiel's hourly rate is quite high."

"It must be nice to have that kind of cash sitting around," another cousin, Demitria, said. "My kids better not need that stuff. We've got a brand new house and a mortgage to pay. No room for singing kumbaya and beating drums, or whatever you're talking about. Kids need to toughen up. They're not all special stars."

"Plenty of kids are very special stars," Tiel said. "They just need people who can help them shine."

"Nope, kids need more discipline. I got the belt, and look at me. I turned out fine," one of the husbands—Stavros-call-me-Stav—said. I couldn't keep track of who went together.

"I think you're doing important work," one of the aunts, Daphne, said. "You just never know what will make a difference, and sometimes you have to try everything.'

Another cousin—I think that one was Irene—pointed at us, wagging her fork. "What about you? You're an architect, so you're building a house, right? You know, for when you're married? You better get to work on having kids soon." She aimed her fork at Tiel. "That clock is ticking, and you're not getting any younger. My neighbor's daughter-in-law waited until she was thirty-two, and ended up spending fifty grand on fertility treatments. They didn't even have a baby; they ended up divorced."

I wanted to snatch every one of those words from the atmosphere and steal them far away from Tiel. She didn't need this woman loading her up with baby anxiety, not when I knew she was already loading it on herself.

And yes, *of course* I knew she was stressed about trying to conceive. Few were those who recognized the perfectionism in her, as they were often distracted by her rambling and rainbow-inspired attire. But I knew there was no prodigy without a thick thread of perfection. Tiel was well-acquainted with hard work, but she was also accustomed to getting good at things quickly.

We weren't getting good at getting her pregnant, not yet.

"We have a house," I barked.

"You live together *now*?" Maybe-Irene asked.

Tiel nodded, and I didn't miss her sharp intake of breath before she spoke. "Yes, we've been living together since the summer."

"Someone get the rosary beads," Agapi muttered. "My mother's about to have a conniption fit."

"Oh my saints," Mrs. Desai said. She closed her eyes and pressed a napkin to her lips. "How did this happen? Where did we go wrong with her, Vikram?"

I knew Tiel's family leaned toward highly religious, but Tiel was a thirty-year-old woman, and a really fucking independent one at that. She didn't require her parents' approval for anything. I wanted to jump in, but Tiel's mother started shouting at her father in Greek. They went back and forth, gesturing wildly and slamming hands, glasses, and utensils like they were punctuation. Everyone else stared at their plates and snuck wide-eyed sidelong glances at each other.

"Great, that's just great," Tiel said under her breath.

Mrs. Desai pointed to Agapi. "Your sister didn't live with Antonio before they were married," she said. "Now, they might have spent a little more time together than I was comfortable with, but he respected your family enough to know better. Agapi didn't let men take advantage of her like you so clearly do. Why can't you find a decent man, Tiel? Someone like Antonio?"

"*Excuse me,*" I started, but Tiel was already responding.

"This has nothing to do with decency or respecting my family," Tiel said. "If that's your argument, you'll have it without me."

I glanced at Tiel, more than a little shocked by the steel in her voice. I definitely expected some of her trademark stress-babble.

"A man who *respected* your family would have asked your father's permission before" —she pointed to the hotly debated pink diamond— "before that happened. If you respected yourself, you'd want that, too."

"I'm going to stop you right there," I said.

Mrs. Desai turned an impatient eye on me. "You seem very…nice," she said. I was now certain that *nice* meant anything but that. "But we don't know the first thing about you. You're telling us our daughter is living with you but you couldn't be bothered to ask her father for her hand before proposing marriage. It's a tragedy. This all sounds like another one of Tiel's New York City plans, and you should both be ashamed—"

"I'm going to stop you again," I interrupted. "Your interpretation is wholly inaccurate."

My hand found Tiel's under the table, and I laced our fingers together.

"Are you a churchgoer, Sam? Which parish do you belong to in Boston?" she asked. "You don't *look* Greek Orthodox to me."

"My mother attended services at Mary Immaculate of Lourdes before she passed away. She preferred the Traditional Latin Mass and I've made financial contributions to ensure that mass continues," I said. "She's interred there now and I visit her grave regularly, but I'm not an active member."

Mrs. Desai sniffed. "You won't find a well-regarded priest to marry you in his church if you're not a member of the parish. And not with this living arrangement. I wouldn't want that in my church."

"It's good that we've cleared this up," Tiel started. "But we aren't planning a church wedding."

Whether this was new information to me was irrelevant; I'd marry this girl on a rollercoaster at Disney World if that was what she wanted.

"If you're not married in a church, you're not married in the eyes of God, and you're not married in *my* eyes," her mother said. "I know you like everything different and non-traditional, with your pink diamonds and piercings all over your ears and all this silly music, but I can't stand by while you have another make-believe marriage."

Mrs. Desai held up her hands and shook her head, and there was no stopping the growl in my throat.

"I can't do it," she continued. "You're inconsiderate, and you're causing your father and I tremendous pain. All we've ever done is sacrifice, and it's never good enough for you. You're giving me angina, you know. I don't know why you do this to me, Tiel. It's selfish. You have to stop thinking of yourself all the time. You're a child playing house with a man who doesn't have the decency to ask your father's blessing, and that tells me everything I need to know about the two of you."

There were babies cooing and crying, interchangeable cousins whispering, and utensils scraping against crockery, but the only sound I could hear was my pulse roaring in my ears.

I squeezed Tiel's hand before I stood, and pulled out her chair.

"Thank you for having us," I said, "but we'll be leaving now."

"I'm going to pray for you both," Mrs. Desai said. "But honestly, I don't think it's going to help. You're impossible, Tiel."

"I'm sorry you feel that way," Tiel said, looking between her parents. Her teeth sank into her lower lip, and she stared at the table for a moment before she stood. "We won't trouble you with an invitation to the wedding."

*Five*

SAM

*November*

THE PSEUDO-GLOBAL-GOURMET CHAIN restaurant near our hotel in Cherry Hill was the only place open, and that alone made it the best port in this storm. It was surprisingly busy for a holiday dedicated to home cooking, and there was something profoundly sad about the assortment of lonely people seated at the bar. Mostly men, mostly middle-aged, all focused on the banks of televisions streaming college football games. They didn't notice me and Tiel, probably because we looked as lost and empty as they did.

There was a dry martini with extra olives lined up for Tiel, and I was staring into a gin and tonic. We hadn't said much since leaving her parents' suburban home, and we hadn't stopped touching each other. In the car, my hand was anchored on her thigh, a narrow attempt at keeping her grounded in the reality of us and away from the chaos of her family. We shared a long embrace while we waited for seats at the bar. My arm was tight around her shoulders now, and I had half a mind to haul her into my lap and promise it all away.

But there was no panacea. Nothing could wipe away the foul film of a parent's loathing, no matter how much liquor you threw at it.

I'd tried and quite roundly failed many times.

"That was probably more than you bargained for," Tiel said, her eyes still trained on her glass. She dropped her head to her hands, pressing her thumbs to her temples and rubbing. "*I'm* probably more than you bargained for."

"Don't start with that, woman," I said. "If anything, we have more in common now."

I tugged her fingers away from her head and brought our hands together, aligning our coffee-stain birthmarks. Mine was a bit worse for the wear after my time in Maine, now shot through with a thin, pink scar from a slippery incident when cleaning some freshly caught fish in the rain.

Tiel's eyes slid in my direction, narrow and unconvinced as she frowned at our birthmarks.

"I told you they weren't going to appreciate the wine," she said.

"There's a difference between not appreciating the wine and your drunk cousin dumping half the bottle into a plastic cup and mixing it with pineapple juice. I felt that like a kick in the balls."

Tiel shifted to study me. "We're finding humor in this now? Really?"

"We're sure as shit not going to sit here and let any of that bring us down," I said, raising my glass and gesturing for her to follow. "To you and me, and our family, and hoping to hell that we don't fuck up our kids like our parents did us."

Our glasses clinked, we laughed, and for that moment, we smiled around the darkness of today's events.

"You pulled the dead mother card," Tiel said, peeking at me as she sipped her drink. "Didn't think I'd ever see you go there."

"The situation warranted it," I said. The server set a selection of appetizers between us. Tiel poked at the dishes, but didn't eat anything.

"Thank you," she whispered. "Thank you for saying those things about me and my work. I'm not sure what I expected but…but thank you."

"Of course," I said as I moved the plates around. Samosas and flatbread for Tiel, ahi carpaccio for me. "But tell me you know that everything they said was complete horseshit. The entire thing, from the second we walked in the door, was horseshit."

"You want to talk about horseshit? I'll give you horse-shit. Agapi convinced my mother she needed to go on the pill when she was fifteen because it would clear up her skin," she said. "She had sex, like, *all the time*, before she got married. With *a million* guys! And yet I'm the slutbag. I was a freaking virgin until I went to college."

"Really? Me too."

Tiel shot me a surprised glance as she nibbled a samosa. "You *are* a piece of something nice, though. That part wasn't horseshit."

"And I'm precious when I hold babies," I said.

"So precious. My ovaries are still turned up to *boom*."

I set my drink on the bar and slipped my hand under her skirt. "Can we capitalize on that?"

"Feed me cheesecake and tell me I'm pretty, and you can capitalize on anything you want," Tiel said with a watery, half-heated smile. "I hear you're indecent and disrespectful."

"That's how my fiancée likes it," I said, laughing, but the humor had left her eyes.

This time I did drag her into my lap. I held her close, my lips on her neck and my arms around her torso, and I wanted to absorb all her pain. Telling her it was horseshit and offering witty observations only went so far.

"Are you all right, Sunshine?"

Minutes passed while she was tucked into my chest, and I didn't expect a response. And I knew the answer: today didn't break her, but it left bruises. How could anyone walk away unscathed after hours of backhanded comments and an all-out shaming session? That we were here, snarking on this afternoon's shiny points, was proof of Tiel's strength. Those bruises would heal, in due time.

"We're not going there again," she finally said.

"No, we're not," I agreed.

"I don't want to be here anymore, Sam. Let's get the hell out of this town," she said. "I know, I know, it's crazy and the drive home is—"

"We'll go to Manhattan," I interrupted. "We can get there within two hours. We'll spend the rest of the weekend in the city, and I'll reach out to that celebrity chef, the one who had the big restoration project in Hyannis. He's got a new restaurant, or two."

Her eyes brightened. "Yes, and now we can go to the theatre! Some of the shows reserve a handful of tickets for day-of sales if you go to the box office, and sometimes they have really good seats. Years ago, when *Rent* was on Broadway, they did this crazy thing where they had a wooden bench all the way down front. You could wait in line each morning to buy these super cheap tickets, and I swear, they were the best seats, and my heart still melts every time I hear 'Seasons of Love.'"

"What else would make you happy?" I asked.

"Can we go to Serendipity for frozen hot chocolate?" she asked. "I've never done it because it's so touristy, but I've always wanted to."

"You're getting all the frozen hot chocolate you can eat, Sunshine," I said.

"Oh, and hotel-room sex is my *favorite*."

"Don't I know it," I said. My phone was out, and I was already searching for rooms with Central Park views. "I intend to fuck you hard enough that you'll black out and forget this entire day. The only memory you'll have is my handprint on your ass."

"You are so good to me," she said, and there was a reverence in her voice that outsized my lewd promises. She needed this from me, and she needed it tonight.

Tiel had been independent for ages—with parents like that, she'd have to be—though there was a part of her, a tiny, fragile part, that wanted to let go. But the lines were fine. Her independence was hard won, and feeling much distance from it put her in panic mode. She would rather make boggy decisions than let anyone rob her of choice.

Hence the tenure-track gig that was steadily killing her passion for music.

The one place I could call all the shots was the bedroom, and it was damn good that we were headed there. She needed to get out of her mind, and she needed to know exactly how bare and exposed she could be with me.

"I'm warning you now, sweetheart," I said, my lips ghosting over her ear. She burrowed into my chest with a sigh. "You won't be able to sit down for a week without thinking of me."

"Thank you," she said against my shirt. "I don't think I could have done all that today without you. You're a special star. The specialest."

"Only because you help me shine," I said.

---

**"OKAY,"** I said, scowling at the traffic ahead of us. "Let's seize this opportunity to talk."

"Seems unwise," Tiel murmured.

The past two days were a blur of Broadway shows, mind-blowing sex, and late nights. Tiel got in touch with some of her New York band geek friends yesterday, and we found ourselves at a massive after-show cast party that didn't wind down until dawn. My head was still ringing from the wine and nonstop a cappella battles, and Tiel didn't look much better. But it was worth it.

"Now that we're headed home and we've gotten all these hurdles out of the way, and we know that we're going to do whatever we want, let's decide."

"Decide what?" Tiel asked, her voice hoarse. She sang the shit out of *Les Misérables* at that cast party.

She sipped her cappuccino and stared out the window, but I could tell from the way she kept her arms crossed and the tight pull of her shoulders that she was still processing the past few days. The detour to New York City helped soothe the sting, but it was a short-term remedy at best.

"Decide what we want for our wedding," I said. I

wanted my tone to be easy and reassuring, but the words came out fast and eager, revealing exactly how desperately I wanted this locked down.

"How are you capable of talking about a wedding right now?" she asked, chuckling from behind her coffee. "We just spent a weekend at The Plaza, drank Greenwich Village dry, and you dropped five *thousand* dollars on *Hamilton* tickets."

"My baby wants orchestra center, my baby gets orchestra center," I said. "My baby also likes it when I fuck her against windows in fancy hotels, so my baby definitely gets that, too. And I want you to give me a single example, outside of this weekend, of the last time you've let me spoil you."

She held up her hand and wiggled her ring finger at me.

"Aside from that," I said. "Listen. I want to give you the wedding you want, and I don't care what it costs."

"Does it have to be a big deal?" she asked.

"It doesn't," I said. "It can be whatever we want. You want to fly to Vegas next weekend?"

She sucked in a breath and shook her head. "No, no, we're not eloping," she said. "I eloped once, and I don't want *this*" —she drew a circle around us as she spoke— "to have any resemblance to *that*."

I grabbed her hand to put an end to the illustrative drawings, and kissed her wrist. "I couldn't agree more," I said. "But 'not eloping' leaves the door wide-open. Do you want the ballroom at Sixty State Street? I know the GM and I'll get it for you. Or a wedding on the beach somewhere tropical? Pick the island, and I'll book the flights tonight. Or a party at one of your favorite hillbilly music shops? Say the word and I'll make it happen. Tell me what you want and—"

"That," she said, shifting in her seat to face me. "The party. I want the party. I don't want a big, serious wedding thing. I don't want aisles or roses or white cakes or invitations with check boxes for chicken or fish. I want it to be fun."

I didn't know how the universe created someone who knew my heart, soul, and abhorrence of all things typical the way Tiel did, but I appreciated the fuck out of those cosmos because this girl was going to marry me.

"Then let's have a party," I said.

She twisted her scarf around her finger for a long moment before saying, "But maybe we don't tell anyone." Before I could protest—she knew that I didn't have many requirements beyond her, but my siblings were non-negotiable—she continued. "I don't mean a secret, but maybe a surprise? Instead of all the formal weddingish stuff, we just have a party and surprise everyone by getting married."

I tapped my thumb against the steering wheel as I considered this.

"And instead of one of my so-called hillbilly music shops, we should do it at home, in the fire engine bays. Everyone would think we're having a little holiday party or something, and it would be such an insane surprise."

When she put it that way, the idea seemed perfectly weird, and I couldn't imagine our nuptials any other way.

"Holiday party?" I repeated. "You'd be good with…next month?"

She drank her cappuccino while I navigated a few miles of traffic. "How about Christmas Eve?" she said. "It's crazy, I know, but think about it—your family always has a

Christmas Eve event, and most of my friends usually stay together for random holiday hijinks. I think we could pull this off on Christmas Eve. Andy might kill me for creeping on her Christmas Eve party because she's been talking about it since August, but I can handle her."

"We'd hire a caterer," I said, giving her a pointed glance so she understood it wasn't an option. Tiel could cook for the masses after growing up in a restaurant, but that wasn't how I intended for her to spend the days leading up to her wedding. "And a decorator to make the garage look better than polished concrete and bricks."

"Okay, but only if we can have little corn dogs."

"Since when are you a fan of little corn dogs?"

She held up her hands as if I was severely missing the point. "I'm not, but nothing says 'this isn't a traditional wedding' more than corn dogs. Oh, and tiny baskets of French fries."

"I can respect that argument," I said. "We'd have to tell Riley. We couldn't plan an event at the house without him noticing, and he won't tell anyone."

"And Ellie," she added. "I know the band has a few days off for the holidays, but they're still overseas. I need her here."

"Only if Ellie can join us," I said, tapping my thumb again. "And Erin, too. We should email her, though, because she doesn't like talking to people. Let's see if her showing up is even within the realm of possibility."

"Okay," Tiel sang. "But first would you tell me what actually happened with her? And Shannon? Why don't they talk? Does she live in Europe because of what happened, or does she live in Europe because that's her life? I mean, we just came from the most fucked-up family situation on the eastern seaboard, but how is it okay for your sisters to be estranged for years? And with *your* family? The people who find sport in seeing how much time they can spend together while also giving each other an epic quantity of shit. How does Patrick not turn on the growls and demand the situation be fixed?"

"I don't know all the details," I hedged, ignoring the part about Patrick solving problems through growling. Too accurate.

"Who are you trying to convince with that? Me or you?" Tiel asked. "Everyone in your family knows everything about everything."

I gestured toward the road, as if the cars and signs and sky could encapsulate the feelings I had about Shannon and Erin's war of silence. The two were surprisingly close-lipped about it all, never amassing allies or inciting skirmishes. While they certainly interpreted moves from any of us as acts of allegiance or treason, their relationship was never open for discussion.

*Ever.*

I scratched my jaw, scowling. "There was a cannonball."

"A cannonball?" she repeated.

"Yeah," I said. "You know how there are little monuments in old town squares and cemeteries around Boston? Where they have a stacked pyramid of cannonballs, and some shiny old cannons or statues?"

"Vaguely," she said.

"Erin stole a cannonball."

"Erin. Stole. A cannonball." Tiel stared at me, her expression packed with skepticism. "Is there more to this story, or are they at odds over the cannonball itself? It's far-fetched but it wouldn't surprise me if your siblings went to war with each other over historical artifacts."

"I believe it was some kind of prank, and she got arrested," I said. "Erin brought the high school baseball team with her, and they took out the entire pyramid of cannonballs. They relocated it to a rival team's field. Home plate, to be exact. They all got arrested, and it was a big deal because the players were disqualified from a state championship game. It was in the news, and…it was a big deal."

Tiel was silent for a beat, her arched eyebrow conveying all of her incredulousness. "Okay. That sounds like a well-executed senior prank with some unfortunate consequences, not the grounds for a years-long cold shoulder. Shannon's tough but she's not ridiculous. And you don't have to share this with me if you don't want to, but you're either not telling me the whole story or you don't know the whole story. Which one is it?"

Too damn perceptive, my fiancée.

"Shannon sorted out the legal shit but basically locked Erin's ass down, and then…things declined pretty quickly."

I paused, not wanting to continue with this topic. A part of me believed that Shannon and Erin would stop what they were doing, wherever they were, and call to rip me a new one because they sensed this topic was afoot and I knew better than to air their dirty laundry, even to my future wife.

"We are climbing all the way up the trust tree right now, Sunshine."

"And in the trust tree we shall stay," she said.

A frustrated grunt rattled in my throat. "The cannonball was the tipping point," I said. "Shannon was really worried about Erin. She was always pushing her to see a therapist, and—"

"Wait, go back," Tiel interrupted. "Why was she worried? Start from the beginning."

I supposed this was reciprocity. I'd seen all of Tiel's family baggage this weekend, and now she was seeing mine.

"My father took out a considerable amount of anger on Erin," I said, and I was aching for the day when those memories didn't turn my stomach. "He hit anyone who crossed his path, but he aimed for Erin as often as possible. The things he did to her...fuck. I don't want to think about it."

"I'm sorry. I didn't realize this was such a thorny topic for you. I shouldn't have pushed." Tiel set her cup in the center console and grabbed my free hand. "We don't have to talk about it."

I'd often heard that it was best to get these things out in the open, to discuss and grieve and process, but fuck if that wasn't the worst idea in the world. As far as my siblings and I were concerned, talking about the heinous shit we survived under Angus was a destination of last resort, but that didn't mean we weren't dealing with it in our own ways. Matt and Patrick exorcised their issues by pounding the pavement, Riley solved all his problems with weed, Shannon was a big proponent of therapy, Erin pulled crazy stunts, and I went on months-long sabbaticals to the wilderness.

No single approach was right, and none were completely wrong, either.

We didn't come together to compare war stories, and not

because we wanted to keep secrets or sweep these horrors under the rug. Some monsters were better left in the closet.

"It's fine," I said eventually. "When Patrick and Shannon finally got Erin out of my father's house, she was not okay."

"But Erin didn't want help?"

"Oh, hell no," I said, laughing. "You can't tell her anything. She does what she wants, and God help you if you get in her way. If you think Shannon is strong-willed, Erin is doubly so."

Tiel laughed into her coffee cup. "How is that even possible?"

"Erin is the vodka-Red Bull to Shannon's whiskey-rocks." I shrugged, not sure there was a better way to describe their fundamental similarities but wild differences. "Shannon became Erin's custodial guardian, and Erin lived with her for about two years. Those were two *long* years. It was like Erin wanted to see how much she could push Shannon, and it turned out that she could push really fucking hard."

I hated thinking about that time. I was away at Cornell, trying to reinvent myself, and Shannon was back in Boston, trying to save the world. A piece of her died inside those two years, and another piece died when Erin left.

"There was the cannonball incident, and Shannon went hard at the counseling angle after that," I said. "And then it got *really* bad." I grated my fingers against my chin scruff until I was ready to continue. "It got really bad, and then it got worse, and then…everything fell apart. Erin fell apart."

"Oh, God," Tiel murmured. "Is she okay? Now?"

"I think so, but Erin works hard at keeping a lid on things. As far as I know, she hasn't discussed this with anyone since she picked up and left Shannon's apartment a

month or two before her high school graduation." I
scratched my jaw again. "Things happened between them
that you can't erase."

I still remembered Shannon's call that day, every word
of it. She was terrified that she'd made the wrong decision,
but even more terrified that it had been right.

"She hasn't spoken to Shannon since. It's going to be
nine years this spring."

"Whoa," Tiel said. "I'm not sure what I expected, but it
was *not* this. Where did she go when she moved out?"

"In with Matt," I said. "Erin stayed with him until she
left for college, and he's the only one she consistently
talks to."

Tiel was silent for the next three miles, then said, "That
was one hell of a cannonball."

# DECEMBER

From: Samuel Walsh
To: Erin Walsh
Date: December 3 at 09:43 EDT
Subject: Looking ahead


Hey, Erin,
I want to talk to you about two things, both of which are
top secret.

First – Tiel and I are getting married Christmas Eve. We're
having a party at our place, and the wedding is going to be
a surprise. You have to be here. Tell me you can make it.

Second – I want to take Tiel somewhere totally unexpected for our honeymoon. It's my wedding gift to her but I'm not going to tell her until after the event. What do you recommend, world traveler?

Let me know.

Sam

------

From: Erin Walsh
To: Samuel Walsh
Date: December 3 at 04:04 GMT
Subject: RE: Looking ahead

Samuel.
I'm amused by your newfound interest in surprises. Surprise wedding, surprise honeymoon.

As far as destinations, no one expects to find themselves in the Chechen Republic.

As far as your nuptial event, my hands are full here in Iceland, with Bárðarbunga.
- e

------

From: Samuel Walsh
To: Erin Walsh

Date: December 4 at 16:31 EDT
Subject: RE: Looking ahead

Erin,
I'm looking for a non-Chechen honeymoon, but thanks for
that suggestion. What about Thailand? Or South Africa?
I've thought about Chile, too.

And I'm serious about you getting your ass here for my
wedding. What can I do to make that happen?

Sam

---

From: Erin Walsh
To: Samuel Walsh
Date: December 7 at 01:55 GMT
Subject: RE: Looking ahead

Thailand: You'd hate it. I happen to love Isaan and Chiang
Mai, but you would lose all your shit after nine minutes in
Thailand. It's not your speed, dude.

South Africa: Cape Town and Johannesburg are killer
spots.

Chile: The Andes and the Atacama are fucking amazing. I'd
only recommend Chile if you're planning an off-road,
outdoors, wild-style honeymoon. You go to Chile to climb

the steppes and pet an alpaca. You don't go there for
couples massages and champagne.

See also: Croatia (I partied there during yacht week four
years ago. Hvar and Komiza are incredible), Marrakesh,
Melbourne, South Island of New Zealand.

Finally: I am not critical to this operation. I appreciate the
invite and I'm delighted for you and the little missus but
me attending your wedding isn't a factor in anyone's happiness. Move along.
- e

From: Samuel Walsh
To: Erin Walsh
Date: December 7 at 21:01 EDT
Subject: RE: Looking ahead

Erin,
You're wrong. Your presence is important to my happiness,
and Tiel's too.

If this is about Tiel, you should know that you'll love her.
I'm not just saying that because I love her. You should also
know that none of Tiel's family will be here for the
wedding. They're not nice people. They think music is a
waste of time and they use religion as a reason to treat her
like garbage, and she needs us to be her family now. I'm not
asking you to be her best friend, but I am asking you to
show up for someone who feels abandoned.

You might know something about that.

If this is about Shannon, I can guarantee that her attentions will be elsewhere. She announced this morning that she's been dating Lauren's brother on-and-off for a year and a fucking half, and they're living together now. Riley, Patrick, Matt, and I took a three-hour lunch at Abe & Louie's to process all of that.

If he's not enough for Shannon, she'll be busy strangling me for throwing a wedding without telling her in advance.

If this is about money, I'll pick up the tab on your flight and anything else you need. I hope this goes without saying, but all you have to do is ask.

If this is about wanting a place to stay that isn't the Matt and Lauren Love Den, there's space at the firehouse. Tiel's friend, Ellie, and her girlfriend, and a few of the people from Ellie's band are also staying, but we have the room.

If this is about something else…I'd love to hear your side of things.

Sam

---

From: Erin Walsh
To: Samuel Walsh
Date: December 11 at 11:54 GMT
Subject: RE: Looking ahead

I'll be there but for fuck's sake, don't make me catch any goddamn bouquets.

And I've known about Will for a year and a fucking half. All you had to do was ask.

- e

*Part Two*

## ...MARRIAGE...

*Seven*

TIEL

## DECEMBER

### I HATED TIME ZONES.

More specifically, I hated that time zones made it impossible for me and Ellie to get on the phone when one of us wasn't running to a sound check or falling asleep. The European leg of her band's tour was packed with performances—they often had two shows each day—and now we were resorting to email.

I hated email, too.

It wasn't our mode of communication. Me and Ellie, we were auditory in nature. When we were together, our conversations were laced with belted-out lyrics and hummed melodies because that was our native tongue.

I wanted Ellie in my ear while I thumbed through dresses because there was no possible way I could choose one without her real-time input. I needed her talking the crazy out of me.

Okay, perhaps I was exaggerating the dress issue. Riley insisted that I'd love the atelier co-op where a friend from RISD was developing a new line of funky formal wear, and that did sound intriguing. Andy and I had a dinner and dress-shopping date lined up for tomorrow night, and I knew I was in good hands with her taste and Riley's recommendation.

Andy knew we were shopping for The Dress, although she didn't know The Day was right around the corner. For all her intensity and precision, she was pleasantly laid-back when it came to operating without complete information. Whenever I told her I didn't know, or didn't want to discuss something, she shrugged and moved on as if it was a non-issue.

I would have given anything for her kind of calm because the crazy? Yeah, that wasn't going away.

I didn't want to feel this way. I wanted to wrap up the fall semester without a bucketful of regret over my complete lack of meaningful research and paltry publication totals. I wanted to find heartfelt Christmas gifts for my future in-laws, and finally succeed at sending holiday cards. And more than anything else, I wanted a taste of the bride experience.

Never once did I believe that walking away from my mother's dining room table would result in a clean break. Oh no, I knew better than that. No repossession of self was ever complete without watching as the roots snapped, receded, shriveled.

And it fucking *ached*.

At first there were voicemails. My father, my sister, my Aunt Daphne. Some of my cousins called, but I knew they were primarily interested in a spin on the drama llama.

I deleted the messages without listening but that didn't mean I wasn't curious. What were they so insistent on sharing with me? Was it anger? Rejection? Sorrow? Or was it something else altogether? Did they even comprehend the reality of it? After all these years, it was possible that everyone else experienced that day as one in a long line of "Tiel, you're a mess!" incidents, and nothing more than that.

There were emails, too, and that was another reason to hate email.

Sam had found me in the showers-turned-studio space at the firehouse last week, fighting back tears as I read a message from Agapi about the pain and anguish I was causing our parents, and it wasn't going to surprise her if one of them suffered a heart attack or stroke and died as a result of the misery I'd inflicted upon them. Oh, and I was a fat, stuck-up bitch with a fake engagement ring.

From that point forward, I handed my phone to Sam whenever I saw notifications from my family, and he read and removed them for me. Most of the time, he offered a quick shake of his head while he scowled at the screen, and that was his way of telling me not to worry about the message.

Instead of worrying, I got swept up in the final weeks of classes before winter break, and tasked myself with building The Best Wedding Playlist Ever. It was all Van Morrison, The Lumineers, Jack Johnson, Neil Young, Ed Sheeran, Ellie Goulding, Mumford & Sons, Corinne Bailey Rae, David Gray, and The Fray. It wasn't enough to create a playlist; I was also obsessed with recording my own versions of these tracks and forcing my syrupy love songs down the unwitting throats of my YouTube subscribers.

But it didn't diminish the phantom limb pain that radiated through my body as the messages tapered off, finally grinding to a halt in the most screeching silence I'd ever heard because I knew it was *over*. I was a train wreck, a disappointment, a cautionary tale, and I didn't belong to my family anymore.

That was when crazy came to town and set up the circus.

Sam had tolerated my ups and downs without much more than an arched eyebrow for weeks. Sympathy shone in his eyes every time I launched into extensive arguments about lazy undergrads or laundry soap that left our clothes smelling of grape juice or our inability to agree on a wedding cake. His touches were longer, deeper, and every day began and ended with him fucking me until I lost the power of speech.

It was his attempt at replacing what I'd lost, at tattooing unequivocal love into every fiber of us until everything else faded away, and I doubted that I'd ever be able to properly acknowledge what he was doing for me. And it was that deep sense of gratitude that held my wobbly moods in such sharp relief. I'd been irritable and impatient and aching, and willing to argue about anything that crossed my path, and he was taking every punch I could throw.

I knew I was funneling my hurt into misplaced anger but it felt like a rock rolling down a mountain, out of my hands and gaining speed and mass until it *was* the mountain, earth and stone and sky all ambling downward until it crashed.

Until *I* crashed.

LEAFING through the mail after the most boring department meeting in the history of department meetings, I stopped when I found a large envelope from my bank. I tore into it, expecting to see new policies and disclosure statements, but found a letter stating that my student loans had been paid in full.

I reread the letter until the words stopped making sense. Eventually, I dialed the number on the top of the page and waited to be connected with a real human person who could explain this madness. She confirmed that the letter was correct, thanked me for my business, and ended the call before I could mumble out a "Thank you."

Glancing around the kitchen, I spotted Sam's phone and keys on the table. Letter in hand, I went in search of him, and stopped first in his workshop before heading to the basement gym. I heard the rhythmic pounding of his feet against the treadmill before I rounded the corner, and if I hadn't been dumbstruck by the dissolution of my debt, I would have admired the graceful coil and stretch of his shoulders, or the light sheen of sweat on his bare back, or his perfectly biteable rear end.

Okay, so I took a minute to admire those things.

"Hey," I said, positioning myself beside the machine and moving into his line of sight. "What is this about?"

Sam squinted at the letter as he slowed to a walk. "Is there a problem?" he asked, panting.

My eyes wide, I looked between him and the letter. "Tell me you didn't."

He reached for a towel and rubbed it over his face and chest before responding. "Do you want the truth," he started, "or do you want me to tell you I didn't handle this?"

"*Handle this*?" I repeated. "I'm something that needs *handling*?"

"Tiel," he growled, his stare pointed. "Stop."

"I'm trying to be calm about this," I said, my voice rising as it quivered. "But here's a list of the things I do not understand right now. First, you stalked my stuff. How did you even find my balance and account numbers? I mean, that's—"

"*Tiel*," he interrupted.

"*Sam*! I'm going to say what I need to say, and then you can be shirtless and sweaty and glare at me with your thick lumberjack arms crossed, but not until I'm finished."

He lifted an eyebrow and leaned against the treadmill. He gestured toward me and then folded his arms over his chest, forcing me to gaze at his taut forearms. And chest. And goddamn it, a shirtless Sam was a weapon of panty destruction. "By all means. Continue."

"Okay, so you have the bright idea to pay off *my* loans without talking to *me*," I said. "What am I supposed to say right now? Thank you?"

Sam shook his head and shrugged, and that gesture tripped me far into the freak-out zone.

"I like doing things my own way, on my own time," I said, and the words were coming fast and frantic, and the sting of accusation was heavy. I knew I needed to throttle back, but I couldn't. I'd fought too hard for my self-sufficiency. I'd worked too long to claim my independence. I'd surrendered so much of myself to this man, and trusted him implicitly, but I didn't want him *keeping* me. "I don't appreciate you swooping in and deciding that you can just... just...*wife* me."

He rubbed his forehead, chuckling. "Are you using wife as a *verb*?"

"That's what you want to talk about right now? Parts of speech?"

"I'm not *wifeing* you. That's ridiculous, and I think you know it. And are you forgetting that we're getting married in six days, and anything that isn't already shared between us will definitely be shared then?" he said, his hand waving at the room. "You're not allowed to have a problem with it."

"I'm not *allowed*?" I shrieked. "You are fucking outrageous right now."

"Oh, I'm outrageous? You're the one acting like we're getting married and starting a family, but we'll live fully independent lives otherwise. Do you think I haven't noticed that you *still* keep the credit cards I gave you in your jewelry box?"

*Oh my fucking God. Not the credit cards again.*

Sam had given them to me after I moved in, and I figured it was like when your parents handed over a credit card when you went to a high school marching band competition in western Kentucky and it was to be used in extreme circumstances only. But when the statement arrived last week, he noticed that I had yet to make any charges. That happened to be the same day he came home to find me mending some fallen dress hems and coloring in a bleach spot on a black skirt with a Sharpie, and he went a little apeshit.

Sam earned a lot more money than I did, and as often was the case with people for whom money wasn't an issue, he didn't see the problem with that. He didn't feel any inequity with what I brought to the table, but I felt it. I hadn't stopped feeling it.

"I don't want to need you," I cried, and I hated those words before I finished saying them. His eyes crinkled as he flinched, and I deflated, torn between tending my pride and soothing the hurt I'd created.

# Eight

SAM

**DECEMBER**

I BLINKED AT TIEL, my arms crossed and my jaw tight enough to trigger a muscle spasm. Blinking was all I could do to prevent myself from darting off this treadmill, throwing her over my shoulder, and marching up to the bedroom, but we'd long since agreed that real issues were talked out, not fucked out.

And this was a real issue. I'd been meaning to discuss paying off her loans because I didn't want it shaking out like this. Unfortunately, there wasn't much in the way of conversational time between us right now. I was knee-deep with my restoration in Brookline and supporting Riley through bumps with the Turlan project, and Tiel was trying to put a lid on this semester while burning off the open-handed slap of her family's dismissal.

Plus planning a surprise wedding and honeymoon,

which wasn't especially easy on fewer than four weeks of prep time.

We stared at each other for several moments before I conceded. Only part of this was about paying her loans. The rest was tangled up in her struggle to believe that anyone would ever be good to her.

Nodding, I said, "I get that you don't want someone taking care of you because all the people who were supposed to do that turned out to be huge douche-waffles, but I didn't do it to have something to lord over you. I did it because I wanted you to have one less thing to worry about right now, and you're going to be my wife. I don't want *my wife* worrying about things I can solve for her."

"Oh, my God," she cried, her fingers knotting around the dark strands of her hair. "You don't even understand why that's infuriating! I was the one who worked for those degrees, and I was the one paying for them. No one else."

*Because you learned a long, long time ago that no one else will take care of you, look after you, treasure you.*

"I'm sorry that I've made you upset or uncomfortable, or whatever you're feeling right now. I should have said some-thing before I did it."

"Yes," she said, still hopped up on her indignance. She was fired all the way up, but as she stood there, hipshot and hands fisted, it occurred to me that this issue was suitably talked out. The next stage was fair game. "You should have."

"Right. That way we could have argued on the front end, and eliminated the element of surprise," I said, scratching my jaw as I stepped off the treadmill.

My fingers curled around Tiel's elbow, and I led her

across the room to the antique pool table Riley brought home last month.

"But that would have reduced the likelihood of you accusing me of 'wifeing' you. I've come to appreciate your assault on the language," I said, smirking as I gathered the skirt of her dress and pressed her chest to the table.

Tiel jerked up and glared at me over her shoulder. "You can't whip out your dick and make this better. I'm upset right now."

"Oh, sweetheart, I know you're upset," I said, pushing her back down. "You've expressed your aggravation. I've articulated my rationale and apologized. Since there's nothing more for either of us to say, I'm going to lick you until you've calmed down, and *then* I'll whip my dick out. Now shush."

With her red skirt bunched in one hand, I drew her panties down and placed them beside her on the pool table. It was a warning: be good or be gagged. She rolled her eyes at that, but there was no doubt in my mind that she'd enjoy nothing more than some aggressive sex and balled-up panties in her mouth.

I dropped to my knees and flipped her skirt over her waist. "So pretty," I murmured, running my knuckle between her legs. She shivered, and her feet edged further apart, but she remained stiff, as if she thought she could carry on this dispute while I ate her out.

That wasn't within the range of possibilities.

My fingertips ran from the sweet, round globes of her ass down to her ankles, and back up again. Leaning closer, I brought my lips to the soft skin of her inner thighs, kissing and nipping until she sighed, and I could almost hear her body surrendering to me.

"You're delicious," I murmured while I licked across her leg. My teeth closed around the curve of her ass, and I smiled as she squealed.

"You're saying that to soften me up," she said.

"I'm saying that because it's true. I don't know how to function without tasting you every day," I said. My fingers passed over her folds and found her clit, and her sighs stuttered into moans. I stayed there, circling her most sensitive spot and biting her legs, until she was rocking back in search of more.

"Sam," Tiel whispered.

My hand dropped to the hollow of her knee, and I inched her leg up. "So beautiful," I sighed as I kissed her pussy. I was taking my time, savoring and scraping my teeth over her skin, and drowning in each of her pleas and hums.

"Sam," she repeated, this time more urgent, more frantic.

I slipped a finger inside her, then another. "Who takes care of you?" I asked.

I heard balls knocking against each other on the table and clattering into the pockets, and Tiel drawing in a breath. "You do," she said.

My tongue traced her slit until it circled that eager little pearl and she drew in a ragged breath. I sucked—*hard*—until her hips were rolling against the pool table and her fingers were clawing at the green felt, and her arousal painted my face and her walls pulsed around my fingers, and I couldn't think of anything but getting her there, giving her this.

"*Sam*," she cried. "Please."

"Are you sure? You didn't want anything to do with me

a few minutes ago," I said. "Tell me you forgive me, Sunshine."

"Yes." Tiel groaned, and I felt the vibration of her words all the way down to her legs. "I can be upset, accept your apology, and want your cock all at once," she said.

I was teasing her now, my tongue only ghosting over her clit, and she was shaking and panting with need.

"You're going to be my wife, and I have to care for and protect my wife. Are you going to let me do that?" I asked. "Please, baby. Stop fighting me. Let me do that for you, Tiel."

"Yes," she cried. "But that doesn't mean I won't freak out about it sometimes. And is this really a conversation we need to have right this minute? Holy hell, Sam, we can talk about this later because I need you to fuck me *now*."

I kept my fingers moving inside her while I attempted to shove down my track pants and boxers with one hand. I was drunk on the taste of her, the promise of sinking into her, the desire to claim her, and couldn't comprehend the noise coming from the stairs.

"There's plenty of room down here for the beer, wine, and barware. I'll show you where to deliver everything. Let's not leave any major prep work for the day of the wedding because I also have catering and floral coming that day. I don't need a traffic jam outside. We're keeping this event clusterfuck-free, boys."

With my pants mid-thigh, my cock in hand, and my tongue on Tiel's clit, I froze.

"That corner over there is good for—Hey Tiel. What's up?"

"Hey, Riley," she said loudly. She shoved her skirt down, blanketing me in her dress. "You're home early. Very early.

This isn't a normal time for you to be here, and oh—hi, hello."

"These guys are going to handle the bar," he said. "Since we're getting a couple hundred cases of beer and wine delivered, we need a place to hide it. What's, uh, what's goin' on over there?"

Tiel's foot connected with my side, and I sent a silent apology to my cock before tucking it back into my pants.

"Hey, Riley," I said as I stood and straightened Tiel's dress.

"Hey," he said slowly.

His eyes landed on the panties forgotten on the pool table, and his wide-eyed gaze snapped to mine at the exact moment I ran my hand over my glistening mouth.

Riley turned to the two burly guys beside him—one of them was choking back laughter and the other was staring at the ground, blushing—and told them, "Give me a minute with the bride and groom, would you? I'll meet you upstairs, in the kitchen."

The men lumbered up the stairs, and Riley stared at the floor while he stroked his beard.

"I cannot wait until your damn honeymoon," he said. "And when you get back, we're revisiting the rules in this house. I shouldn't be the only one who has to wear pants at all times."

"Put it on the calendar," Tiel said. "Family meeting to discuss pants."

"Done and done," I added.

"You're both too fucking chipper for me today," Riley said, shaking his head. He pointed to the ceiling. "I'm going to handle the preparations for your wedding, assuming George and Geoff aren't too traumatized."

Tiel chuckled. "I think they'll be fine."

"So if you're going upstairs," I said, "does that mean we have the room for a bit?"

Riley glowered at me. "Go right ahead," he said. "But you should know I've had sex on that table, too."

Tiel and I stared at the table while Riley's feet thundered against the stairs.

"So…" I gestured to the green felt and then shook my head. "We'll continue this conversation upstairs."

"Absolutely."

*Nine*

SAM

DECEMBER

THE SUN WASN'T YET PEEKING over the horizon, and as I walked through darkness, frost-covered grass crunched beneath my boots. The early morning chill bit at my face, and I had to force away the uncomfortable knowledge that nothing was safe from the cold here.

Life was easier when I wasn't confronted with death.

My arms were loaded with miniature evergreen trees and gardening supplies, but instead of stopping to set these materials on the ground, I gulped down a knot of emotion as I stared at the tombstone.

The notion that grief faded with time? It was inaccurate. No, grief and loss never faded. Absence never quite abated. It lingered, and sometimes it flared, but it never faded. That was the price we paid for the memories that lived on.

"Hi, Mom," I said.

There were leaves to rake and a rosebush in need of

pruning, and those tasks kept me busy while I gathered the rest of my words.

"I'm getting married tonight, Mom," I said while I mounded mulch around the rosebush. "Although it doesn't look much like a wedding. I guess that's the best part: no one knows it's a wedding."

I set the trees on either side of the tombstone, and then rearranged them three times. There was nothing left to do, but the words I wanted to say were stuck.

Nothing about this day was traditional, and it was possible that we'd unintentionally veered hard into anti-wedding territory. Every time there was a discussion of wedding details, "fuck tradition" was the battle cry and chorus, and that prevailed through it all.

Save for one small exception: I hadn't seen Tiel since last night.

We'd gone to Sligo's, where Ellie's band put on a last-minute performance. All it took was one Instagram post hinting at their location, and the venue was packed beyond capacity. I'd known that her band was thriving, but the turnout was overwhelming. Ellie's girlfriend, Alexandra, only chuckled at my shock and explained their European shows were selling out *arenas*.

The music continued late into the evening, and when the venue finally kicked us out, we made our way to the South Street Diner where Ellie and Tiel took turns sharing wedding performance horror stories.

And Tiel said my sense of humor was dark.

It started with Tiel describing a wedding where she and Ellie performed in a string quartet, but the groom came down with a case of cold feet—Ellie, Alexandra, and the six band dudes all turned pointed glares in my direction at that—and they were forced to play for two hours while the not-so-happy couple argued in the rear of the chapel.

And the stories only got worse—can't-look-away worse —from there. The hung-over best man who puked on the groom's back. The couple that wanted "Pour Some Sugar On Me" as their recessional song, and all the others who requested the *Star Wars* theme song. The springer spaniel ring bearer who plowed down the beachside aisle, took out the minister, and went chasing after a flock of seagulls. The groom's ex-girlfriend who crashed the ceremony to object, and was promptly heckled by the groom's family. The bride who said yes, then no, then yes again.

It was almost cathartic, dredging up the best of the worst from their "two broke band geeks" period, and laughing them away because it alleviated the pressure of this day. As non-traditional as we wanted this wedding to be, it was still a *wedding*, and one fraught with stressors. Cobbling together an event with less than four weeks of prep time. The element of surprise. Tiel's family—or lack thereof. Turning our home into a youth hostel.

When we returned to the firehouse, pancake-drunk and exhausted, Ellie was quick to yank Tiel away from me.

"I'm minding your purity tonight," Ellie said to Tiel.

Tiel wrapped Ellie in a tight embrace, their cheeks pressed together and their eyes squeezed shut. "There's not much left to mind," Tiel said. "The prepster's taken it *all*."

"Get your freckled ass over here, prepster." Ellie reached for me, and then we had Tiel giggling and sandwiched between us. "This should be wrong on every level, but somehow it isn't."

"Hey!" Riley called from the stairs. He bounded down

the steps in nothing more than his loose Batman pajama pants and tackled us. "I want the snuggles, too."

"Okay, *now* it's wrong," Ellie murmured from somewhere under Riley's arm. "Dude. I'm in your armpit. That's not okay."

"What are you talking about?" Riley asked, tightening his hold on us. "I'm delightful."

"It's still an armpit," Ellie cried as she wiggled free. She pointed to his pajamas, and the dick peeking out of the front opening. "I knew I felt something on my leg. Put that thing away."

"Jesus, Riley," I said. "Can you keep it in your pants for a bit?"

He shuffled his bottoms back into order, and jerked his shoulder. "He's friendly. Can't blame him for wanting to say hi."

Ellie then pulled Tiel into the recently constructed rooms we'd assigned her and promised to look after the bride-to-be until the ceremony.

I'd forgotten how to sleep alone. I couldn't make sense of the bed without Tiel nestled beside me, and it felt too big, too empty. Nothing was right, and I must have resembled an anxious old dog, circling and circling in search of comfort until surrendering to inadequate fits of restlessness and dreamless sleep.

The last time I'd awoken, bolting up with a strangled grunt and blinking at our room until I remembered Tiel was in Ellie's care, I gave up on the endeavor altogether. That was when I decided to go to the cemetery.

The evergreens didn't look right, and I adjusted them again. "I've been thinking about this a lot," I started, "and I hate that you're not here, and you won't watch me marry the most amazing woman tonight. I hate that you don't know Tiel. I hate that I'm standing here, talking to grass and stone and forcing myself to believe you can hear me because I *need* you to hear me today. I hate that you left before I was ready for you to go."

My gaze cut to the side, in the direction I worked damned hard to avoid every time I was here. It was a game that my mind played: if I didn't see it, I didn't have to think about it.

About *him*.

Angus.

My father.

No amount of wilderness therapy could erase the mark he'd made on my life, but staring at his grave didn't send my anger into overdrive anymore. His was a basic tombstone, adorned with nothing more than his name and the years of his life, and it simply *was*. It didn't stand as a monument to my misery.

I turned back to my mother. "The last thing you said to me was that I'd be all right." I swallowed the tension swelling in my chest. "And I didn't believe that until now. Not really. I didn't understand how that could be possible, but I think I've figured it out now. I think I know that I am. That I'm all right."

---

"THE CATERING IS HERE and set up, and *delicious*," Riley said around the Sharpie cap between his teeth. "I've had a bite of everything, and I approve. Okay, yes, I ate an entire tray of corndogs but they said they brought extra."

He was checking items off his list while I paced in the

hall. The house was filling with our friends and family, and the band was playing a song that I recognized from Tiel's incessant humming but could never name.

"What's the story with that cake again?"

"It's not a cake," I said. "It's a watermelon carved to look like a pink layer cake with meringue frosting, with twelve tiers of French macaroons on top of it."

"Right. I'll let you explain that to people," he murmured. "My guy from Newport has the two bars prepped, and three bartenders at each. Even for this crowd, that should be enough. And Gigi's almost done with the little alpine and manzanita trees, and—"

I stopped short and whirled around. "Magnolia Gigi? Tell me Magnolia Gigi is *not* here."

He glanced up, and if his impatient glare wasn't enough, his arched eyebrow and hipshot stance told me how much he appreciated my question.

"She's not staying," he snapped. "I told her she should, but she said she didn't want to upset you or Tiel."

"Oh, thank God," I said, scrubbing a hand over my face.

"You need to make that shit right," he said. "She didn't do anything wrong. You're the asshole in this situation."

"Great. Of course. I'll deal with that when it's not my wedding day, okay?" Riley offered a flippant shrug in response. "Would you care to explain to my wife-to-be that instead of talking her off whichever ledge she's climbed out on today, I'm going to smooth things over with Roof Garden Girl? *Really?* I'll sort this out with Magnolia after my honeymoon, but right now? No. No, Tiel is the only woman I'm worrying about today."

"It's fine," Riley murmured. "I told her to charge you double anyway."

"Perfect," I said. "Are there any other women who I've wronged or crises to address, or can I get back to convincing Tiel to go through with this?"

He glared at me again. "Like I was saying, the little trees are almost done and all the lights are strung. I checked in with Ellie when she and the band were setting up, and she said everything is fine on that front. I asked her if they'd play some Kendrick Lamar, or some of Drake's sexy stuff, but she said no."

"I'm sure it will be great. They're pretty good at what they do," I said, turning on my heel to resume pacing. "Is the officiant here?"

Riley paged through his notebook, nodding. "Tiel's friend? Yeah, he's unique. He's wearing a feather boa. What are the odds he's a pimp?"

I shook out my cuffs and glanced back at him. "He's a drum major. There's a difference."

"I'm gonna have to trust you on that, boss," Riley said. He flipped through the pages and looked up, gesturing to his list as I returned from the far end of the hall. "I think we're good. We have food and drink, some flowers and trees, a drum major pimp, a plaid-shirts-and-beards band, and the people. We're good."

I patted my chest, confirming—again—that I had the rings. "Is Erin here yet?"

"Oh, yeah, Rogue's on her way. She's been texting me since she landed three hours ago. Matt and Miss Honey are delivering that package, which reminds me," he said, and then scribbled a note. "She needs supervision. Maybe the bar boys can handle her. All six of them."

Bringing my fingers to my forehead, I groaned. Erin usually went by the nickname Little Mermaid—which she loathed—though Riley stayed strong with Rogue. In this situation, he was probably right. I'd begged her to show up, but I also knew the odds of her getting wild were high.

"Jesus, fuck. Please don't let her start anything. No fiascos. No throw-downs. Nothing," I said. "Didn't she hang out with Nick last summer? At Matt's wedding? He's good when we give him tasks. Let's put him in charge of Erin."

"Nick's my boy, but..." Riley scowled around the pen cap. "I wouldn't trust him with a ham sandwich."

"I don't know what the hell that means, Riley."

"Nothing. Stop worrying. Worst case scenario, I'll lock her in Tiel's studio for the night. She's like ninety pounds. I can take her," he said. He pulled a white square of fabric from his back pocket and handed it to me. "I borrowed it from Matt. It's the one he had when he got married. I know this whole thing is unique, but we should have *some* tradition."

I turned the delicate handkerchief over, my thumb brushing the wrinkled edges and embroidery.

"It's Mom's," Riley added. "I thought you might want it. It's okay if you don't."

"Yes— Right— Yeah— I know," I said. "Thank you. I...Of course I want it." Emotion balled in my throat, and I swallowed against it. "Thank you for doing that."

"No sweat." He reached for my bowtie, no doubt skewing the perfect symmetry I'd achieved, but I didn't mind. "Got the rings?" he asked.

"In my pocket," I said.

Riley nodded, and tugged my lapels. "Good. I'll wrangle the natives. You get the bride. We'll have a wedding."

He stepped around me and started down the stairs. "Ri," I called. "Thank you for all of this."

"Not a problem," he said.

"And Riley?" I called. "What the fuck are you wearing? And when was the last time you had a haircut? Or shaved?"

He glanced down at the kilt and shrugged. "I lost a bet," he said, leaning toward me with a smirk. "But I think I actually won, because this thing is awesome. My balls are ecstatic. I would legit wear it every day, and chicks dig beards. Man-buns, too."

I shook my head with a sigh. He had the Jason Momoa-Brock O'Hurn man-bun going, which was significantly better than the stubby ones I'd seen on many a pretentious asshole in recent history. And his junk wasn't falling out of his trousers, and that was worth celebrating.

"I don't even know how to respond to that." Eyeing the crowd again, I said, "Shannon just walked in with SEAL Team Six. Go distract her."

She was going to wring my fucking neck when she realized this was my wedding, and she'd been enlisted as neither consultant nor coordinator.

"Roger that," he said. "And please note, we're calling him Captain America."

"Fantastic," I muttered. "I need a goddamn flowchart to keep up with this shit."

I knocked on the heavy barn door that separated our bedroom from the surrounding area, listening for any sounds of protest. I didn't know how far she wanted to take this whole 'not seeing the bride' thing.

Tiel hadn't taken the traditional route when it came to anything wedding-related, but it wasn't going to shock me if she pulled out some last-minute request or superstition. She'd been oscillating between hearty bouts of self-confidence and hysterical dips into emotional quicksand since our trip to Jersey, and part of me expected *something* unexpected in order to get married tonight.

If that was even happening.

It wasn't a thought that owned much credence, but there were split-seconds where I read Tiel's anxiety as doubt. But when I pulled back and examined it all with a skeptical eye, I knew it was the toll this month had taken on her. She'd been through a lot with her family, was still contending with a not-so-great fit in academia, and made a point of choking down some foul tea each morning at the off-chance it helped us get pregnant.

The tea alone was a lot to handle. That shit smelled dreadful.

"Sweetheart?" I called, glancing around our room.

A long row of brick arches ran north to south, and we'd fashioned them into alcoves for bookshelves, makeshift closets, and open-air dressing rooms. I found Tiel at the far end, seated on the floor with her back to the brick and her knees tucked to her chest. A tiny plume of peacock feathers was woven into her hair with narrow braids, and she held her dress to her chest, the zipper gaping open at the back. Her hands were painted with swirling designs in ultra-fine henna. Ellie must have initiated that for she was the only person who fully understood Tiel's need to embrace certain elements of her father's Indian roots.

"It's almost time," I said. "Everything's in place, everyone is here—"

"Everyone?" she repeated, her head tilting up to look at me. Her eyes were filled with sad hope. "Everyone, but not..."

I'd sent Vikram the date and location on the off chance he had any balls whatsoever, but my email received no response. He'd stopped messaging Tiel about her mother's broken-heartedness, too, and that was for the best.

I couldn't imagine any member of her family making an appearance tonight, and as she blinked up at me, her bottom lip trapped between her teeth, my heart hurt for her.

"This is about you and me, Sunshine. Nothing else matters," I said, dropping down beside her. "You have me and I have you, and we're everything we need."

"My parents aren't coming to my wedding," she whispered. She was gazing at the floor, her eyes distant and her voice broken. "My father isn't going to walk me down the aisle and my mother isn't going to straighten my dress, and —and *they're not coming* for me. They're not coming for me, and I still don't understand what I did wrong. What did I do, Sam?"

"Don't ever say that. You shine too bright for them, Tiel, and they don't understand you. Don't ever say you're not enough." I brought my arms around her and pulled her into my lap, but she was already shuddering with sobs. "I want to give you everything, anything. My family, my name, my children, *my everything*. Take it all. Take *me*, and let *me* give you everything they couldn't."

She cried into my chest for long, aching minutes, and the only thing I could do was hold her.

"I want all of that, but what if…" Her voice trailed off as she ran a finger up and down my lapels, that bottom lip white against the pressure of her teeth. "What if something happened to you? You're all I have left, and this is serious now. What if something terrible happened? How would I… what would I—"

"Stop," I said, squeezing her close to me as she sniffled. "Stop, sweetheart. Nothing is happening to either of us."

"No, but what if you're walking down the street some day and get swallowed by a sinkhole, or one of your properties comes crashing down around you, or if you got sick and I lost you, and maybe we shouldn't do this. I love us right now. I don't want to lose us. I *can't* lose us."

"Is that what you're worried about? Us changing?" I asked.

She shook her head. "I'm worried about everything, Sam. What happens if we're not the same anymore? If everything changes and you decide you don't want me anymore?"

"This," I said, pressing my palm to her heart, "isn't changing."

"Don't make this about my tits," she said, an anxious laugh catching in her throat. "They're going to get old and saggy. They'll be less entertaining, and you won't love them anymore."

"I will love them always. I will love *you* always." I ran the backs of my fingers along her collarbone. "We don't have to do this if you don't want to. We can go down there, enjoy the music, have some drinks, and—"

"I need to know this won't change anything because I can't do this and then watch it fall apart. I can't be left behind again. I am alone in this world, Sam. I have Ellie, and you, and that's it. I'm afraid I won't survive if you left me."

My arms went around her again, crushing her as a wave of warmth spread out from my chest, down my limbs, around us. I loved this woman harder than I could comprehend. "I regret that this seems to be new information, but nothing will ever keep me from you. Do you believe that?"

Her head bobbed against my chest. "Maybe. Sort of." She looked up, shrugging. "People don't like hanging on to me, Sam. There's a long list of people who have left me, and I'm scared you'll realize I'm not enough of something. I just don't understand why you want *me*."

"And I don't understand why you want *me*, but let's take the next two weeks and work out some lists. Maybe bullet points starting with *I'm a better man because of you* and ending with *I won't imagine my life without you right here, always, and I'm not fucking leaving you*. And something about you being the funniest, sweetest, most beautiful band geek I will ever have the privilege of loving in the middle."

A small smile blossomed on her lips. "My list would start with *you understand me even when I don't understand myself*, and end with *you showed me how to love myself and never complain about reminding me when I forget*. And something about you wearing a red fucking tuxedo to our wedding, and looking like a hot piece of something very nice doing it."

I leaned down to meet her eyes. "Then come with me now. Come be my wife."

---

IT WAS A DARK, unholy hour when the party finally started winding down, and that was only one of the reasons I was pleased as fucking pie that I got a room for us at the Four Seasons on Boylston. It seemed frivolous to spend this much on a Public-Garden-view suite when I owned a fully decent firehouse on the other side of town but...but we got *married* tonight.

Something—*everything*—about that demanded opulence.

And a guarantee that little brothers wouldn't be barreling in with random questions about the whereabouts of his swim fins, or whether anyone wanted an omelet while the stove was hot.

"This is so fancy," Tiel whispered, squeezing my hand in the elevator.

She glanced at the bellman and back to me, a goofy, slightly drunken grin on her face. The peacock feathers that were once artfully woven into her hair were listing at an odd angle, and her eye makeup was smudged, but all I could see was perfection. I mean, we were both fucked up three ways to Thursday, but this—this night, us, right now—was the start of something good. Something perfect, in its own wildly imperfect ways.

I brought my hand to her face, my palm cupping her cheek while a tight part of me breathed a sigh of contentment as she leaned into me. Edging forward, I pressed my lips to hers for a quick, soft kiss. "You're fancy," I said against her lips. "This dress is gorgeous. And really fucking hot."

The elevator came to a stop, and we followed the bellman down the silent hallway. He was probably bursting with questions. It wasn't as though many people checked in during the earliest hours of Christmas morning, and far fewer showed up in red tuxedos or peacock-inspired dresses with miles of crinoline puffing up the skirts.

So I put fifty dollars in his hand, asked him to hang the Do Not Disturb sign, and engaged the dead bolt and chain.

When I turned back to my bride—*my wife*—she was gazing out at the Garden, her hands braced on the windowsill and her ankles crossed. Shrugging out of my jacket, I smiled, and let the deliciously loose, liquid sensation that belonged to a tangled mess of love, affection, and peace fill my chest and simultaneously ease one form of tension and stoke an entirely different one.

I draped the jacket over the sofa's arm and toed off my shoes, my eyes never leaving Tiel. I walked toward her, wondering what she was thinking as she stared at the grounds below. Her head was cocked to the side, her foot shook in a lazy rhythm, and what did I do right in this life to deserve her?

I didn't know, and I was more than half certain I didn't deserve her at all.

The only reasonable solution to that conundrum was fucking her against the window.

Bow tie, cufflinks, shirt, belt, glucose monitor: off.

Trousers: unbuttoned.

"It's ridiculous to expect a white Christmas," she murmured, inclining her head toward me but not looking over her shoulder. "There's never snow this early. It's always January and February, but there's this huge anticipation for it. All this snowy excitement, as if snow makes a Christmas more valid or something, but when you think about it, it's summer in the southern hemisphere. They don't have white Christmases. It's an irrational expectation propagated by western civilization, right?"

"I'm sure we can blame Dickens for that. We'll get to it when we're back from our honeymoon," I said, my hands resting on her hips. "Did you have a good night, my love?"

"Mmm," she sighed, leaning against me. "It was incredible."

I shifted her hair over her shoulder and dropped my lips to her neck as I unzipped her dress.

I was waiting for some qualification: incredible except for her family's absence; incredible for a thrown-together, last-minute wedding; incredible if we pretended that Lauren didn't drink her weight in shots and challenge the bar boys to arm wrestling contests; incredible aside from the fact that Nick was seen throwing Erin over his shoulder and carting her from the firehouse shortly before we departed.

"Really, really incredible," she said. She reached back and roped her arm around my neck. "I can't believe we did it. We pulled it off. We're married now, Sam. Like…*married*."

"Having second thoughts?" I asked. I drew the dress down her body, helping her step out of the dark teal silk with subtle hints of gold and silver woven into the delicate lace overlay. It left her in bright pink panties, a matching bra, some off-kilter peacock feathers, and the diamonds I put on her finger.

She threw a sharp glance over her shoulder, shaking her head. "Of course not," she said, her brows furrowed. "Do you think it will be different? Will *we* be different?"

"Give me your panties, and we'll find out," I said.

I wasn't ripping these. No, some things were worth saving, and wedding day panties were one of them.

I locked my gaze on her eyes while she shimmied out of her bra and panties. It was the only safe spot. If I looked at her tits, I'd want my tongue on them. If I looked at her legs, I'd want them wrapped around my waist. If I looked at her ass, well…things would get out of hand quickly.

She placed her underwear in my outstretched hand, and I gestured for her to face the window again. I tucked the fabric into my pocket for later, dropped my trousers and boxers, and gripped my cock. I jerked slowly, letting the head slide over her ass and into the warm, waiting heaven between her legs, but I didn't thrust forward. Not yet.

Part of me wanted *everything* to be different, and it made me feel like a motherfucking caveman.

I liked it.

I wanted my cock to literally rise to the challenge of consummating this marriage and claiming this woman as my wife. I wanted her pussy to hum with the knowledge that it was all mine now. Really, truly mine, and not simply because we loved each other or shared a bed, but because we'd made promises, commitments, vows—and not just the ones we'd shared in front of our friends and family tonight.

But another part of me, the part I knew Tiel was grappling with, wanted everything to stay exactly the same. We'd worked our asses off to find *us* and make *us* work, and now that we were finally getting good at *us*, changing it up came with a dose of terror.

"I love you," Tiel said. Her hips rocked back, and I slid against her slippery skin. "Nothing will change that. I love you. My filthy pervert. My best friend. My husband."

I crowded her up against the window, her breasts pressed to the glass, my hand sliding down her leg to grip the back of her knee and my mouth on her neck, and I was so deep inside her I couldn't discern what was mine and what was hers, and I didn't need to because it was *ours*. We were an *us* now, a *we*, and there was no point at which she stopped and I began. I bit and sucked and swore and *thrust thrust thrust*. I covered her mouth with my hand when she tripped into that high, screaming wail that I coveted like my personal g-spot merit badge.

Tiel arched away from the window as she came, and she took me with her.

Staring out at the Garden, we lingered there, panting, sweat cooling on our skin, touching. When the shudders and shocks subsided, Tiel led me to bed, plied me with a bottle of orange juice, and reconnected my glucose monitor. She ran her hands through my hair, over my shoulders and chest, and checked the device every few minutes until the numbers started climbing back into normal territory.

I nestled my head between her breasts, dragging my tongue over her skin and loving the taste of her. My wife.

"So…" Tiel scraped her nails over my scalp. "Should we talk about Nick and Erin now, or is that a conversation for another time?"

"Oh, hell no," I said, sighing against her chest. "I'm going to lick your tits and enjoy my life, and not get involved in any of that. Good plan?"

"Great plan," she agreed. "Happy Christmas, my husband."

Happy. There was that word again….but now?

Now I knew happy's story.

I married happy.

I lived happy.

I owned happy.

"Happy *everything*, my wife."

*Ten*

JANUARY

I DIDN'T KNOW where the term *honeymoon* came from, or what it meant before it was converted into the modern day model of tropical bliss and sex under gauzy mosquito nets, but our honeymoon didn't fit that characterization.

On the one hand, that made sense for us. Spending a week day drunk and lazing on the beach in Hawaii or me flattened on the deck of a sailboat while Sam fished off the coast of Cozumel wasn't in our cards. No, that wouldn't do. We weren't getting in line for the standard-issue honeymoon when the wedding was Mumford & Sons-meets-Van Morrison.

But then again, after thirty-six hours in the air, three flights, and one particularly thorough customs inspection upon arriving in Australia, the standard-issue honeymoon sounded just fine, thank you. There was also a late visit from my period—nope, still not pregnant—and freak thunderstorms and flash floods that left the city of Melbourne rain-soaked and cold for days.

Instead of sunset walks along the shore or some frisky underwater groping, we listened to downpours and hail battering our hotel while the power flickered on and off. Oh, and we were on each other's very last nerves.

Cranky old married couple status achieved.

Melbourne itself was amazing—our bitching and bickering owed nothing to this beautiful city. But everything was soggy and we were beyond exhausted, and the combination of my cramps and Sam's more-erratic-than-usual blood glucose meant we were too wrung out for more than room service and *The Lord of the Rings* trilogy.

When the sun appeared on our fourth day in Melbourne, we dragged ourselves out of our Federation Square hotel. We were going to see the sights, eat the food, and enjoy the culture, damn it.

The Montalto Vineyard and Olive Grove was nearly two hours away, but the quiet ride down the Mornington Peninsula gave us time to drink in the scenery as it morphed from city to suburb to rural.

As the highways thinned and the trees thickened, I found myself filled with frustration over everything and anything. This wasn't *me*. I didn't travel halfway around the world to nap. I didn't argue with my husband about plot holes in *The Return of the King*. I didn't whine about Australia's slight variations in bagel baking. I didn't celebrate pulling off the greatest surprise in Walsh family party history by grousing about puddles and rain clouds. And I didn't let something like not getting pregnant this month ruin my one and only honeymoon.

That goddamn tea. I should've known the old traditions weren't working on me.

When we arrived at Montalto, we were treated to an extensive tour of the property, starting with the vines and ending with the cellar door and production areas. Sam photographed everything and asked questions as if he was preparing for a quiz at the end. Always studious, my Sam.

"Do you want to eat?" I asked, hooking my thumb over my shoulder in the direction of the winery's restaurant when the tour guide departed. "Or do you want to see the sculpture garden first?"

"Neither," he snapped. He made quick study of the cellar, and pulled me down a shadowy row of racked barrels. We stopped at the far end, and Sam crowded up against me, backing me against the rack. "You've been somewhere else all day, and you've barely said a word. I want you to tell me what the fuck is wrong."

"Nothing," I said, and it sounded hollow even to me. "Let's sample some of that wine, then lunch, then the sculpture garden."

Sam braced his hands on either side of my shoulders. "Are you happy that we're here? That we did this?" he asked. "Getting married?"

"Yes, *of course*," I said resolutely. "Happy isn't even the right word. I'm overjoyed, and I wanted this to be perfect. *Everything*, perfect. But I'm annoyed with myself because things haven't been perfect, and I've let that bother me but we're *here*, in this awesome place, and that's all that matters. And..." I looked up from the precious patch of skin at Sam's open collar to meet his eyes. "Are you having regrets?"

His hands fell to my shoulders and spun me around,

and he was hiking my long, gauzy skirt up to my waist. "Fuck, no," he growled.

Sam's foot pushed at mine, widening my stance as he rocked against me. He was hot and hard through his trousers, one hand cupping me over my panties while the other roughly palmed my breast. His breath was coming in heavy puffs, like a bull growing impatient with his matador, and that impatience was multiplying by the minute.

I gasped when his hands fisted around my panties and the snarl of ripping fabric rang out, but I wasn't surprised that he tore them. I would have been more surprised if he merely edged them to the side, or took some other, less primitive approach.

"I fucking love you, Tiel," he said. The force of his unzipping had his loosened belt clanking against my bare backside, and I arched away from the cool slap of metal.

"Oh, fuck," I cried, a gasp taking hold of my words and carrying them away as he thrust inside me.

Sam's hand shifted from my breast up to my neck in warning. *Be quiet or I'll keep you quiet.*

"Oh, my God," I said, turning my face into his arm to muffle the noise. "Your cock feels huge."

"That's because you haven't had it all week." His palm settled over my mouth and he shifted to speak into my ear. "This is going to be fast, my love. Hold on."

His hips snapped as he drove into me again, and with the all-over pleasure came relief. This was the kind of sex that brought tears to my eyes. Not because it was profound or beautiful—although I was sure it'd be hot as fuck to stumble upon some angry sex in a winery—but because it uncapped all the tensions mounting between us and let them spill over until they ran dry. This kind of sex took everything I had and boiled it down to grunts, thrusts, moans.

Then he eased back, nearly pulling out, and lingered *right there*. His hand was splayed low on my belly, his finger offering only a hint of pressure on my clit, and this state of desperate, aching need sent those tears spilling over. "Please don't," I sobbed. "Please don't leave me."

"As if I could," he said around a groan.

Panicking at the loss, I layered my hand over his and pressed back. My body bowed at the heavy drag of him inside me, and I was right there, liquefying under his touch.

"I need— I need—" I hiccupped against the hand covering my mouth.

He drove into me, the force propelling me forward until I was clinging to a wine barrel for support.

"Ah, fuck, Tiel," he said, his mouth on my neck and hips bucking, wild and erratic. He groaned into my skin as he came, and then he shifted, his hips still undulating as he wrapped his arms around my torso and jerked me as close as any two people could get while half-dressed and fully fucking in a dark wine cellar. "I know, sweetheart, I know."

The thunderous punch of my orgasm was rolling through my body, all heady aftershocks and emotional tidal waves, when he brought his head to my shoulder and stilled while his cock pulsed inside me.

"Sam," I murmured. I couldn't find any of the words I wanted right now, but more than that, I required the safety of his arms and the bonds of his embrace. He nodded—he felt it, too, and he needed it as much as I did. "I love you, too."

"We should probably buy a case of wine," he said, laughing as he glanced around. "Maybe two."

Sam rained kisses along my neck, ear, and jaw as he pulled out, and the absence left me whimpering. "Your cock really did feel huge."

Dropping to his knees, Sam brought my shredded panties between my legs and gently wiped away the evidence of his release. "My poor, pervy girl." He pressed a kiss to my core before standing, righting his royal blue trousers, and tucking my undies in his pocket.

I pointed to his pocket. "That wasn't very nice."

"Oh?" he asked, a grin pulling at his lips. "I thought it was outstanding."

Rolling my eyes, I shifted my skirt back into place but the damp spots had me cringing. "You know what I'm talking about." I waved at my clothes. "When you rip my undies at home, I can get another pair. But we're *here*, and now I'm a mess. I'm all—you know—*wet*, and I have to walk around like this for the rest of the day."

"Let that serve as a reminder that you need to talk to me," he said, and fire was back in his eyes. "Total honesty, my wife."

I ran my fingers through my hair and adjusted my clothes again, nodding. "And that goes quite well with food," I said when I finally met his eyes. "And wine. We should sample some of it before you buy a case. Or two."

We spent the remainder of our time Down Under exploring the local arts scene—my heart was overflowing with live music—and incredible eateries. The entire city pulsed with a culture so vibrant and diverse that we were gobbling up every garden, gallery, and artsy laneway by the armful.

Sam went hog-wild for the Flinders Street Station clocks, and had full-on architecture boners every time we turned down a new street or discovered another gorgeous park. One afternoon, Sam was so enamored with one nineteenth-century home that he insisted we ask the owner for a tour. He turned on all the Sam Walsh charm, complete with enough incendiary smiles to melt bricks…and panties.

The little old lady who answered the door not only invited us in, but also served us lunch and dragged out a scrapbook tracing the home's history back nearly two hundred years.

Sam was in architect heaven, and he was sharing that heaven with me.

It was all I *needed*, but there were a few more things I *wanted*.

# Part Three

## ...AND EVERYTHING AFTER.

*Eleven*

SAM

## FEBRUARY

I SPRINTED to the attic conference room on the thin hope that I'd bought myself a few minutes with the tribe before Riley caught up with me.

"Listen up," I said when I reached the landing. Patrick, Matt, and Shannon turned toward me. "I hid Riley's hot sauce on Tom's desk. We have three or four minutes, max."

"Yeah, that's exactly what we need," Matt said. "He's a pissy bitch if he doesn't have hot sauce with his breakfast burrito."

"I'm aware of that," I said. "Seriously though, he's freaking out about Turlan. He's not going to ask for help, but he needs all of us, all week."

"Is this intended as new information?" Patrick gestured to the color-coded project management spreadsheet. "I've already planned for everyone to be on site, supporting the wrap-up work at that property."

"That's not the point," I said. "It's that he doesn't need to think we're expecting him to fail. We need to show up for him, and not give him any shit about it, either."

Riley's voice boomed from the stairwell. "Fuck you very much, Thomas. How'd you like it if I borrowed your almond milk? No? You wouldn't enjoy it if I decided to help myself to that creamy nut water you call milk? Then don't kidnap my sriracha, sir."

He stomped up the stairs, grumbling as he made his way to his chair, a bottle of sriracha and a foil-wrapped burrito cradled in the crook of one arm, his laptop, notebook, and water jug in the other.

"How's it going, RISD?" Matt asked easily.

"Fantastic, Jugger, fuckin' fantastic," he said. "The Bruins lost last night. I dropped my coffee on the goddamn sidewalk just now. Your assistant stole my sauce, Mrs. Halsted." He pointed at Shannon with his burrito. We were all still miffed about her no-invites wedding. "That's punishable by death in some parts of the world."

"Probably not," Shannon said.

"Where's Andy?" Riley asked. He clutched the bottle to his chest like a security blanket. "She'd agree with me on this."

"Home," Patrick said, his eyes cutting to the iPhone beside his laptop. He tapped it to life. "Stomach flu."

"Is that code for pregnant?" Matt asked. "I mean, half of us are married now, and even if you haven't sacked up and made it legit with her, it wouldn't be illogical to expect some babies around here soon. You know, mathematically speaking."

"Tryin' to tell us something, Jugger?" Riley asked as he tore into the burrito.

Matt shook his head as a chunk of scrambled egg broke free from the tortilla and tumbled to Riley's leg. "No, dude. Just...a question," Matt said, staring at the fallen clump of egg.

"And your attempt to dismiss my question raises my suspicions," Riley said.

"Focus on your food," Matt said, gesturing to Riley's trousers.

It was a sore spot, that I knew, but a shamefully envious part of me roused to life at the thought of Patrick and Andy or Matt and Lauren having babies before me and Tiel. We'd been trying, and that no longer included the simple pleasure of lots of sex. Now it was tracking her vagina's moods —that was what she called it; she hated the term 'cervical fluid' and with good reason—and triangulating her most fertile days and abstaining on her less fertile days in order to jack my sperm into a frenzy.

I could abide any quantity of cervical fluid and peeing on ovulation monitoring tests, but I wasn't fond of the abstinence. I'd now taken to giving my sac pep talks when it was go-time, ordering my swimmers to do their fucking job.

"No." Patrick glanced at his phone again, swallowing. He cleared his throat. "Moving on. The only priority that we have this week is Turlan. It goes without saying" —he pinned me with a purposeful gaze— "that we are all hands on deck until the open house and media showcase on Saturday. Walk me through your issues and priorities, Riley."

Last night, Riley and I'd inventoried the Turlan jobsite and jotted down all the action items we needed to hit this week. I'd prepped him on how to present that property's status, but he was hesitant. There was something about discussing delays and problematic new developments that stung of failure and inferiority, and he was a pro at avoidance.

But this time, he paged through his notebook and launched into an accounting of every paint smudge and loose hinge on the site, all while devouring a burrito the size of my forearm. That boy knew how to eat.

Patrick blew through each of the issues, deftly delegating them around the table until the only remaining items involved the PR and event planning, and that was Shannon's ballgame.

"Here's the final attendee list for Saturday," she said, handing a folder to Riley. "Give it one more look. Make sure we're not missing any important vendors. I haven't been able to keep up with which ones you've fired. You're worse than Patrick with that itchy trigger finger of yours, RISD."

Patrick rolled his eyes at that, and launched into a status review our other properties, Riley paged through the list, and his expression shifted from indifferent to confused. Project talk quieted and all attention tracked toward Riley as his otherwise easygoing demeanor turned *furious*.

He tossed the folder to the center of the table and sat back in his chair, his arms folded over his broad chest. "Why the fuck is one of the lead designers on this project not on this list?"

*Here we go.*

Shannon grabbed the file and scanned the list. "I've been over this list forty-seven times. Who are you talking about?"

"Magnolia is the principal landscape architect, and she designed and installed the roof garden, but since we're a band of assholes who won't forgive mistakes, she's not coming." He pushed away from the table, his scowl deepening. "If assholes could fly, this place would be an airport."

"I'm not sure what you want me to say." Shannon stared at the file, frowning. "We haven't told her not to come."

Riley turned an irritable glare in her direction, his head shaking slowly. "Maybe not, but she slaved over the motherfucking roof garden and she obviously doesn't feel welcome at the fucking showcase because we're fucking dickholes, and that shit needs to stop."

I was the fucking dickhole. It was all me.

The problem was that I liked Magnolia. And yes, I cared about her in the most professional manner possible. She was talented and imaginative, and I admired her work. Our relationship was one of mentoring, and that was based on my desire to see her succeed. I didn't mind offering her constructive feedback on her designs, but I hated informing her that her advances toward me were unwanted and inappropriate, and we couldn't work together if she had romantic feelings for me. I didn't want to sit down over coffee and revisit her unrequited affections for me or how those affections led to me and Tiel hurling the most hurtful words at each other that we could find. I didn't want to put her in an embarrassing situation like that.

"That was an exceptional quantity of profanity," Matt said. "Impressive."

Riley responded with a fist bump across the table. "I'm serious," he said. "This needs to be solved, and it needs to be solved right fucking now. This thing that we're doing— where we're blowing Magnolia off because she had some weirdness with Sam—is bad business. To be honest with you cuntcakes, I thought we were better than this. I didn't think we operated this way. It's petty and immature, and this isn't the kind of business we do."

They weren't the cuntcakes. I was the cuntcake.

"Cuntcakes aside," Matt said, "maybe we should reevaluate. I'm not involved in the day-to-day with this project, but showcasing without the landscape architect doesn't sound right to me."

"Can I ask whether your concern for Roof Garden Girl is more than professional?" Patrick shrugged. "To be clear, I agree with Matt, but your pleas are quite impassioned."

Riley dropped his head to his hands, muttering something about being the only sane one in this family. He looked ready to chuck that bottle of hot sauce straight at Patrick's head.

"Do I understand this correctly—I'm only allowed to treat a partner with respect if I want to fuck her?" Riley asked. "And not that it matters, but Gigi has a boyfriend who is not me."

"That's not what I said," Patrick replied.

Riley shook his head, unconvinced. "It sure as shit sounded like what you said."

"All right," Shannon interrupted, her palms extended between Patrick and Riley, "I'll handle it."

He pointed at me but kept his gaze on Shannon. "*Sam* should handle it, but at least you're not going to pussyfoot around the situation until shit's gone sour."

---

**Sam:** How's your afternoon, Sunshine?
**Tiel:** Let's not talk about that. Tell me good things
**Sam:** What's wrong?
**Tiel:** Nothing. I've just had undergrads in my office, bitching about their grades all damn day

**Tiel:** I got an email from someone's mother asking me to reevaluate an essay grade

**Tiel:** It took 100% of my willpower to not respond "are you FUCKING kidding me?"

**Sam:** Wow

**Tiel:** Yes. Exactly.

**Tiel:** But please…tell me good things

**Sam:** Riley and I are meeting with a staging crew later in the afternoon, but I can grab some Thai food. We have a new episode of *Outlander* to watch

**Tiel:** Hell yes. I love everything about that show and I'm going to read those books as soon as I make tenure my bitch

**Sam:** There's the Turlan party this weekend

**Tiel:** I'm super worried that I'm going to embarrass the entire world when I meet Eddie Turlan.

**Sam:** Unlikely

**Tiel:** Ummm, have you met me?

**Sam:** You will be perfect

**Sam:** I think Magnolia is going to be at the event too

**Tiel:** Of course. She did the roof garden, right?

**Sam:** Yeah, I just wanted you to know. I didn't want it to be a surprise.

**Tiel:** It's not a big deal, as long as she doesn't try to steal you from me

**Sam:** I can't be stolen.

*Twelve*

TIEL

FEBRUARY

THIS MEDIA SHOWCASE wasn't fancy, it was *elegant.* Tuxedos, formal dresses, valet outside, champagne and crystal stemware inside, and punk-rock-royalty-turned-eco-conscious-hipsters in every corner.

The dress I was wearing cost more than the monthly rent on my old apartment, and I was standing statue-still with my hands knotted in front of me because I was convinced I'd trip and cause a series of red-wine-spilling events otherwise.

I hadn't wanted a new, spendy dress that I'd only wear once, and initially thought one of Ellie's would work for the grand unveiling event at the Turlan restoration, but that idea didn't fly with Sam. He sent me to Neiman Marcus, and dispatched Shannon to assist in my shopping.

Interestingly, that endeavor wasn't awful. The most complicated part was looking at the prices without throwing up in my mouth. And hanging out with Shannon —just the two of us, for once—was fun. The last time we'd been together without some other wife, girlfriend, or Walsh within arm's reach was that afternoon when Sam was on his wilderness adventure and we'd squared off in the coffee shop. Almost a full year had passed us by, and in that time, everything had changed, even us.

In a sense, we were different people now: her Shannon Halsted, and me Tiel Walsh.

Shannon had badgered me into selecting a long, full-skirted dress with a bright, abstract floral pattern. It was the most wonderful thing I'd ever seen, but the price tag was terrifying.

In addition to my not-causing-mayhem project, I was also working hard at keeping an open, neutral expression on my face while Sam chatted with a reporter about this home's sustainability features. That wouldn't have been too difficult if I didn't have to watch one legendary musician after another move through the brownstone and not glom all over them or squeal like a crazed fangirl.

"Do you want some wine? Champagne?" Sam asked when his interview wrapped. His fingers ghosted down my back, and without thinking, I sighed into his touch.

"No," I said, laughing. "I'm not risking it. I'd twitch and you'd be dripping wet, and that wouldn't be good for anyone. And bad things happen with me and fancy champagne."

"Great things happen with you and champagne." Sam leaned into me, laughing. "I love your misplaced anxiety. You're not clumsy, but put you in a spiffy dress and an upmarket house, and you make it seem like you routinely cause catastrophes."

I spared him a glance, one that I hoped said *I cause plenty of catastrophes, thank you*, but he was staring at my cleavage. He was looking hard, his eyes moving as if he was working through something complicated in his head, and his tongue darted out, painting his upper lip.

I knew that look. It was the one that usually led to shredded panties and reddened, tender bums, and often involved a request to come on my tits. It wasn't completely unwelcome. I loved knowing that my husband was addicted to me, and anyone who complained their husband's sexual appetites were bothersome was either lying or working with a man who didn't know how to use the tools.

Mine was real good with the tools.

But we had at least another hour at this shindig, and we weren't sneaking off to a dark corner of this house. Not with more than one hundred people here and a swarm of media.

Glancing around the room for a diversion, I spotted Shannon and her new husband, Will. He was smirking at her while she spoke, and that took a special edition set of brass balls. But that wasn't the most fascinating thing I noticed.

"Your sister," I murmured, nudging Sam with my elbow. "She has pregnant boobs."

Sam's head was still bowed toward my breasts as if exercising his right to public worship, and he grimaced before leaning into my ear. "First, I don't want to talk about that. Second, she's devout when it comes to the pill, and I only know that because she used to set an alarm to take it during morning meetings. But that meant she was running downstairs to get her bag, or snoozing the alarm only for it to go off every five fucking minutes until the meeting ended. We put it to a vote last year, and made her reschedule the thing. And finally, what constitutes *pregnant boobs*?"

I shrugged. "I can't explain it but I just *know*, Sam. It's a gift. Some people can pick race horses, I can spot pregnant boobs."

"You're sure it's not a push-up bra or something?" He kept his gaze fixed on me.

I glanced at Shannon again, and noticed the rosy glow high on her cheekbones despite the wintry chill in the air tonight. She looked good. Healthy. And her otherwise small breasts were busting out of her dark plum dress.

"She's pregnant," I said, turning my attention to Will. "Look at those two. They don't even need to have sex. There's a cloud of hormones around them. All he needs to do is give her a hard look. *Boom*. Pregnant. I guess some guys are gifted like that."

I realized the impact of my words as Sam stiffened. A muscle in his jaw flexed while he absently stared over my shoulder and silence choked the air around us.

"Sam, I—" I stopped.

"I know what you meant," he said quietly. "It's fine."

If it was fine, he would have laughed and offered a quick comment about Shannon and Will's inseparability, or their thoroughly entertaining love-hate. The Walsh kids rarely articulated the things that rubbed them the wrong way, instead pelting each other with sarcasm and quippy remarks like a take-no-prisoners game of paintball. Shannon's whiz-bang relationship was the preferred playing field at the moment.

The boys were all feeling a bit pouty over their lack of

involvement in Shannon's personal life of late. It was precious how they handled the turn of these tables.

"Maybe we should..." My voice trailed off as I saw Shannon and Lauren moving toward us. "We should talk about all of that. In the trust tree."

"We should," Sam said. "Let's see what happens this month, and then we'll go tree climbing."

"I *am* sorry," I whispered as Shannon and Lauren were steps away. "You have big, beastly, hearty lumberjack sperm."

"Do lumberjacks swim well?" he asked, his lips pressed to my temple. "Sure, they can demolish your forest but they might not be swimming across your bay."

"Hey," Lauren said, pointing at me before I could respond to Sam. I was biting my tongue to keep all the filthy lumberjack comments to myself. "I need to talk to you."

Confused, I glanced around. "Me? Why? What did I do?"

Shannon—with her totally pregnant boobs—pointed at Sam and then gestured across the hall. "The reporter from *Estates* wants a few minutes with all of us."

"Be good," Sam whispered, kissing my temple again.

"I need advice," Lauren said when Shannon and Sam were out of the room. "Music education advice, for my school. I want to get some time with you. When can we have a conversation about that?"

"Um..." I didn't know what to say.

"I'm sorry," Lauren said, touching her fingertips to her forehead. "That was really formal and strange considering you're one of my best friends. I'm in super-crazy-fundraising mode, and keep forgetting to turn it off. Let me start again. I want to hear everything you have to say about kids and music education, and I have tons of questions. Would that be okay? Like, you and me, not during drunken pedicures, not during lunch where everyone's talking at once."

It didn't matter how many journals published my research or how many degrees I earned, I didn't think I'd ever feel like an expert on anything other than the best bagel shops in town.

"Yeah, sure. Anytime you want," I said, still not convinced that I'd be terribly helpful. "Give me an idea of what you need so I can pull together the right research and resources. I'm more useful when I have some time to prepare."

In other words, I rambled like the town fool when I was put on the spot. There was a reason I spent four hours preparing lecture notes for one hour of class.

She lifted her shoulders, her face pulled tight in uncertainty. "Big picture: I think I want to run an early strings program."

I sucked in a breath and pressed my hands to my cheeks. "Oh, my God. Early strings changed my life. That's no exaggeration. I would be the grumpiest waitress in New Jersey if it wasn't for learning the violin when I was little, and no, it's not for everyone but it taught my brain how to listen and think, and I'll do anything you need."

"I want to find a way to make it happen," she said. "I need to figure out the logistics, and I need your wisdom. When would work for you?"

We toggled through our calendars to find the best day to meet. I couldn't look at my calendar without a stir of dread in my belly. It was a buffet of meetings and more meetings, and I hated every one of them. They never offered new information that wasn't also common sense (*à la* don't fuck your students), and they rarely resolved any of the ongoing issues (the curious case of whiteboard markers vanishing from the classrooms). Add to that some heavy-duty contempt for any music therapy methods that deviated from academia's directives, and downright condescension when it came to pop music in therapeutic settings, and I rolled my eyes hard enough to give myself headaches in these meetings.

And calendars did a splendid job at reminding me when we'd know if that hearty lumberjack sperm took down the forest, crossed the bay, *and* yelled "Timber!"

I'd given up on the tea—and good grief, that stuff was horrid—but now I was all over vitamins, supplements, essential oils, and charting. Ellie instituted a forever-long ban on discussing fertility and baby-making with her, and she was known to hang up immediately if I brought up the particulars. Apparently, I was making vaginas unappealing to her.

"Huh," I murmured, casting a quick glance around the room when I finished blocking the time on my calendar. "There's free food and alcohol. Sounds like something Nick would enjoy, right? Is he stuck at the hospital tonight?"

She nodded. "Nick would be all over this. He'd probably bring a baggie or two to save some snacks for later. He does that every time he eats at my house. I don't think that boy has a single pot, pan, or plate in his apartment. But...he's in Ghana," Lauren said with a hint of awe. "It's a Doctors Without Borders gig. He's there for a couple of months, and then he's up for another brief tour over the summer. That one's in Central America, I think."

"Wow," I said. "That's...amazing. I don't think I could ever pick up my life and move to a foreign country for a few months like that, and do all kinds of incredible work. If you told me I needed to teach violin to kids in Ghana, I'd be a disaster. I'd be more harm than help, and spend all my time looking for some decent coffee and bagels."

Lauren murmured in agreement. "All the creature comforts." She took a sip of her drink. "He's been talking about doing it for as long as I've known him. It didn't work for his fellowship schedule until now, but I also think the travel bug jumped up and bit him. He's spending a few days in Morocco and southern Spain before heading back home."

I wanted to ask if she knew anything about him and Erin. I couldn't be the only one who'd seen them arguing— yelling, storming off, chasing after, and repeating the process—at the wedding, and I knew others had seen him scoop her up and carry her out of the firehouse when the party was winding down.

But there was one thing I knew to be true from the short time I spent talking with Erin last December: when she was ready to invite me in and share her side of things, she would. There was no rushing this girl.

"Okay, we know where Nick is, but where's Andy? Shouldn't she be here?" I asked. "Or did I miss her somehow?"

Will was walking our way, and he shared a quick chin lift greeting with Lauren before nodding at me. "Tiel," he said.

"It's always disconcerting to see you in clothes," I mused, surveying his dark blue suit. To me, he'd always be the dripping wet guy with an inadequate scrap of terrycloth covering his bits and bobs who'd answered Shannon's door months ago. "I just assume you only wear towels."

"So wrong," Lauren muttered. "Andy has food poisoning." She shook her head, grimacing. "It's been pretty rough for her. She hasn't been to work all week, and she's *never* sick. I went over there this morning, to their apartment. We talked for a couple of minutes, and we watched *Fixer Upper*, but she fell asleep halfway through. She hasn't kept anything down in days."

"Oh, God," I murmured. "That's awful."

"Yeah but she's tough," Lauren said. "I'm slightly more worried about Patrick, actually. He had a tiny nervous breakdown when I was leaving. I don't think he's slept much this week."

"That's no fun," I said. "I'll have to bring them some orzo. That always settled my stomach when I was a kid, and at the very least, Patrick will eat it."

Will muttered something under his breath, and Lauren drove her elbow into his side.

"Judy is still pissed," Lauren said to Will. "You're ranking below Wes right now."

He stared into his beer bottle, his ring finger tapping against the glass. "Judy will be fine," he said.

"Oh really? Did you see the blog post?" Lauren held up her phone. She glanced at me as she navigated her browser. "Our mother has a travel blog, and it's turned into a really big deal. After she heard that Will and Shannon got married without inviting *anyone*, she reposted all of her photos from the trip she and our father took to Montauk a few years ago."

Lauren handed me her phone as Will rolled his eyes.

The post featured beautiful photos of the village and beaches, and sassy captions.

"See that?" Lauren pointed to a block of text at the bottom. "That's where she sweetly slams Will for eloping in the Hamptons. 'The closest thing I have to priceless memories of Sailor 1's wedding are these old sunny shoreline snaps. The Commodore and I can only hope we're invited to visit Sailor 1 and our new daughter-in-law—we'll call her Ginger—someday soon.'"

Will squeezed his eyes shut and rubbed his forehead. "Motherfuck," he rasped.

"You're in so much trouble," Lauren said, and she sounded downright giddy.

They continued sniping at each other while I watched guests flow in and out of the kitchen. From this vantage point, I could see straight through the great room and into the front hallway, and that was where I spotted Magnolia.

I'd known she was attached to this project, and Sam mentioned that we'd see her here tonight. Since this project was in Riley's hands, he was the only one who had regular contact with her, plus their sporting events.

I watched Magnolia from across the room, shocked that my memory of her was a wild distortion of reality. In my mind, she was everything—sexy to the $n$th degree, skinny but somehow curvy, too, tall and graceful, glammed up, and gorgeous. But seeing her here, now, I realized that she was just a girl trying to fit in, just like me. She was tugging at her skirt and gingerly patting her hair, and looking around with an anxious wrinkle in her brow, as if she wasn't sure what to do with herself.

Months ago, during our big, honest conversation, Sam and I had talked about the whole incident involving her. I understood his perspective, and I accepted and appreciated that he hadn't wanted to embarrass her by calling out her flirting. I would have also appreciated him telling her that he had a girlfriend, but that was in the past and we'd moved on.

Except…I hadn't moved on. Not all the way. I mean, I'd moved, but not far enough that I couldn't still see where I'd been before.

"I'll be right back," I murmured, although Will and Lauren were deep into comparing where they each ranked in their trio of siblings.

Marching toward Magnolia, I struggled to find the right opening line. Part of me knew it was time to do this and it didn't matter if I was a babbling mess while I did.

"Hey," I said, coming to an abrupt stop at her side. Too loud, too perky, too wide-eyed, and way too much stiff smile. One word and I was all kinds of awkward. "Would it be okay if we talked? For a second? Privately? I'm Tiel, by the way, in case—"

"Oh, I remember," Magnolia said, her cheeks pink and her eyes cast down. "And yeah, sure, of course."

I gestured between us, drawing an invisible box that I subsequently mimed grasping and shaking, although I knew this was a terrible way to express our need for a quiet, isolated space. "Is there a room? Like, one that isn't being used for all of this—all of these activities—"

Eddie Turlan's hands landed on my shoulders as he shuffled behind me to access to hallway. "Pardon," he murmured.

I squeaked, a tiny, repressed scream held in check by the fear of embarrassing my husband at this massively posh event. I was certain that my face was melting from that sweet second of contact with a real music legend. The gift in this moment was not only gaining a story to tell for decades to come, but also my complete lack of fangirl screams. This was what adulting looked like.

"What about one of the pantries? Off the kitchen?" Magnolia asked, waving over her shoulder. Her eyes were darting from me to the floor, and she was ignorant to my very real Eddie Turlan Experience. "There are some big closets upstairs, too. Oh, and the cellar, but the last time I was down there, I got a face-full of cobwebs and a big spider was stuck in my hair. And yeah, I work with gardens so I'm cool with spiders and all of God's creatures, but not in my damn hair. So the cellar is *not* my favorite location here but now you're probably thinking that's the perfect spot for this little chat."

I blinked at her for a beat, not sure I understood all that. "You said something about the kitchen, right?" She nodded, pointing in that direction with her glass. The force of her movement sent liquid sloshing over the sides and onto my dress.

"Oh, holy spunk trumpets," Magnolia panted, her eyes impossibly wide. She used the cocktail napkin she'd had wrapped around the base of her glass to pat my dress. It didn't help.

"Why don't we find that pantry?" I asked, stepping away from her frantic hands.

Magnolia looked up at me, her lips parted and her eyes shining with trepidation. "Okay, yeah. Just follow me."

She led us toward a back room off the kitchen, past the catering crew and the wall of champagne cases, and it was suddenly very quiet when the door whispered shut and she turned to face me.

Time to put this girl out of her misery.

"So listen," I started. "I was in the middle of losing my mind the last time I saw you. I couldn't hear any sense or logic that night, and I want you to know that we're good. Really. I know you're close with Riley, and that's—"

"I have a boyfriend," she cried, her hands flying up and waving at the empty shelves.

What was left of her drink was now soaking my chest and torso, but she was too wrapped up in what she was saying to notice.

"I'm not using Riley because I couldn't get Sam, or anything absurd like that. That's not me. I don't even think I'm smart enough for that kind of trick. We just like arguing about sports. I like sports. I know, plenty of girls don't, but I grew up with brothers and someone always had to play outfield. But I've been seeing my boyfriend since last summer, and we live together, and I'm not out to bag a Walsh. I've made some mistakes and lost a really mean-ingful professional mentoring relationship with Sam, but that's what happens when you convince yourself he's just playing really, really, *really* hard to get, and there are times when I think back on everything and I'm like, Wow. I'm not that bright." She shook her head with a groan. "I'm so sorry, Tiel."

"It's all good," I said, and it was the truth.

I didn't need to carry around slightly bitter jealousy when it came to Roof Garden Girl. I got the guy. Such that he couldn't look at my tits without conjuring some indecent thoughts, I was keeping the guy, too. Not to mention he was the most loyal man I'd ever met.

But…tits. They were my daily affirmation that I had this man on lock.

"What?" she asked, her brow wrinkling with confusion. "I meant what I said. I'm honestly very sorry, and now that this project is finished, I won't be seeing Sam at all anymore. Not that I've been *seeing* him, but—"

"Magnolia," I said, "I get it. You work with Sam, and Riley, too, and it was a mistake. It happened, it was bad, it's over, and life goes on. You're going to keep working with the guys, and I'm sure you're still going to games with Riley, and *it's all good*. I trust Sam, and I'm not going to freak out if he sees you because we all know he's married. No more mysteries in that department."

Her hands dropped from where she had them suspended between us, still mid-gesture, and frowned. "Oh," she whispered. "Thank you for being, you know, *not* crazy. That's refreshing."

I shrugged, and took a breath to think about what I wanted to say. This pantry was spectacular, and I was definitely going to bug Sam about building something like this at the firehouse. "It's taken me a fair amount of time to be *not crazy*." I smoothed my hands down my skirt and glanced up at her. "Look. I'm sure I'll see you around, and I don't want that to be weird. I don't want you to assume that I'll force you into the spider dungeon, or anything terrible like that. And maybe you'll stop throwing drinks at me. That's no way to make friends. We'll be *not crazy*, and it won't be weird."

"Not crazy. Not weird," she vowed. "And I'll keep my hands off the Walsh boys."

"Mouth, too," I added.

For a split second, I thought I'd strummed that chord too soon. But then Magnolia laughed, saying, "Adding it to the list now."

"Perfect," I said with a smile. I pointed to the door. "I should get back out there."

"That's a good idea," she said.

We went our separate ways—not without a supremely strained moment where we exited the pantry but then walked in the same direction, side by side, for thirty seconds, not saying a word. We kept peeking at each other and forcing smiles until I "remembered" that I needed to visit the ladies' room on the opposite side of the house.

When I returned to Lauren and Will, I saw Shannon, Matt, and Sam at the other end of the hall. It looked like their interview was finished, and they headed straight for us.

"I'm ready," Shannon said to Will, a hand pressed to her abdomen.

"What's wrong?" Will asked. He pulled her close, folding her under his arm and pressing his lips to the crown of her head.

"I don't know. My stomach feels off, and I want to go home," she said. "I think I'm getting Andy's food poisoning."

"Then say your goodbyes, peanut," Will ordered. "Five minutes, and then I'm throwing you over my shoulder."

"Sweetie, I don't think it's contagious," Lauren said to Shannon. "Patrick doesn't have it."

"I want some sparkling water and my pajamas, and I don't want to analyze the origin of my belly ache," Shannon said, a slight whine creeping into her voice. "And don't you dare hurry me, commando. I'm done when I say I'm done, and your meathead ass isn't carrying me anywhere."

Sam appeared, his hand settling on my waist. We stepped away from the group, moving just beyond the immediate conversation. He lowered his lips to my ear, and whispered, "It would be wrong to tear this dress off, right?"

"You may *not* tear this dress," I said. "I'm not even comfortable wearing something this expensive. Ruining it would be insanity. I'm going to keep it, and tell stories to our grandchildren about the time their grandfather insisted I buy a dress roughly the same price as a low-end used car. It will be a little family folktale, and I'll show them the dress, and they'll ooh and ahh all over it. Or, I could make miniature quilts out of the dress, and hand them down to our children and their children as heirlooms."

"Right, so here's what I heard: dress intact, panties ripped, ass slapped."

I glanced up at him, smiling coyly. "I'm not wearing any panties."

MARCH

"AFTER A YEAR and a half of work, I think it's fair to say that we're all pleased to change the status on the Turlan project to *complete*," Patrick said, and a chorus of agreement went up around the table. "But there's another thing we need to handle with that property."

"If you tell me they want even one more change," Riley said, "I will eat my goddamn shirt. Then I'll move to Brazil and live among the people of the rain forest. At least they won't demand that I re-stain their floors five times."

"Don't eat your shirt yet," Patrick said. He stepped away from the table, and returned with a large paper-wrapped frame. "This arrived Friday afternoon, but I wanted to wait until we were all together." He placed it on the table and held out his hand to Riley. "Open it."

With a heavy sigh, Riley started tearing the protective covering. "We should really get an intern or someone who can open your mail for you, Patrick, because this is a little —" His voice vanished as he took in the four-page spread in *Homes New England* featuring the extensive project.

"The magazine hits newsstands today," Shannon said.

Riley leaned in to read the text, his arms crossed over his chest and his brow wrinkled. He didn't say anything for several minutes, instead studying the up-close photos of his intricate plaster and tile restorations, and sweeping shots of the kitchen and parlor.

"This is nice," he mumbled.

"*Nice*?" I repeated. "It's fucking incredible." I stabbed a finger toward the layout. "You did this, RISD. And you see that? That section titled 'In the Blood'? It says in no uncertain terms that you kicked this restoration's ass just as well as any of us could, and maybe better."

"There are three more articles running in the next month," Shannon said. "Plus several more interview requests coming your way."

"Sam designed Turlan," Riley protested. "Matt did all the structural. Patrick managed the entire timeline, and I don't even know what the budget was on that property. I didn't do anything. The credit doesn't belong to me."

"That's okay," Patrick said. He moved the frame off the table and leaned it against the brick wall. "For what it's worth, your version of not doing anything was damn good, and you should do it more often."

Matt pointed to the magazine spread. "You can hang that in the office you never use. Remember? The one you had to have?"

"Fuck you," Riley muttered. "And for the record, I'm in your office because you always pay for lunch."

"Like that's going to continue," Matt said, laughing. "If

you're running projects like that one, you can afford your own meatball subs."

"All right, moving—" Shannon pressed her fist to her mouth and sucked in a breath through her nose, her free hand curled around the edge of the table. "Moving—" Her voice caught in a sharp gasp.

"Shannon…" Patrick leaned back in his chair and studied her. "Everything okay?"

"Yeah, I'm—" Her shoulders jerked forward, and she waved her hands in front of her face. "All good."

I caught Matt's eye, and he shook his head, mouthing, "I don't know."

"You're sure?" Patrick asked.

"Definitely," Shannon murmured, but then she shook her head and pushed away from the table.

She started to say something, but her words were obscured by unmistakable gagging. She darted toward the tiny washroom tucked into the corner of the attic. She tried to close the door behind her, though it gaped open, leaving us an audience to her distress.

"I'm out," Riley said, holding up his hands in surrender. "I'm sorry. I can't do puke. I'm a sympathetic vomiter. I'm gonna go build some shit."

While Riley gathered his things, Andy collected a box of tissues from the windowsill and headed to the bathroom with Patrick hot on her trail.

"We should—" I started, glancing toward the far side of the room.

"Yeah," Matt said. "We should."

We wandered across the room, all the while feeling as useful as a drawer full of dull knives. "We're here to help," I said when Patrick and Andy noticed us approach.

"I've got this," Andy said, gesturing toward the door. "All of you: finish the meeting, and I'll get her home."

She stepped closer to the bathroom, but Patrick wrapped his hand around her waistband and dragged her back. "You just got over major food poisoning," he said, weaving his arm around her torso, "and you are not taking another step."

Looking down, I stared at my wingtips for a minute while Patrick recounted the gory details of Andy's brush with listeria. She was all right now, after several weeks of recuperation, but she'd lost a substantial amount of weight in the ordeal. The outbreak was linked to some question-able cheese. Patrick instituted a ban on all food trucks and festivals until further notice, and forbade all varieties of basement-cultivated cheeses.

While the food-borne illness discussion did terrible things to the twitchier parts of my brain, I was more fasci-nated by their show of affection. In the two years they'd been living and working together, I'd never witnessed a true Patrick-and-Andy moment in the office before. Sure, there were light touches and inside jokes and all those non-verbal conversations that none of us understood, but they kept it exceedingly professional.

More painful retching echoed from the bathroom, and Andy pivoted in Patrick's arms. "I'm completely fine, and she needs someone right now. I can't stand here and not help her."

Patrick walked Andy back toward the conference table, and said, "Do not come any closer. If you'd really like to help, go to your office. No, no. Go home and get some rest. I can't handle seeing you suffer again."

He kissed her forehead and murmured something I

couldn't hear. She shook her head and gestured in obvious disagreement, but he held her hands to his chest and spoke into her ear until she started nodding. After a long embrace, she collected her things from the table and headed downstairs.

Patrick returned to our uncomfortable gathering and knocked on the door. "Does your husband know you're sick?"

"Shut up," Shannon groaned.

"I can call Will," Matt offered as he reached for his phone. "Although he'll probably answer by telling me that he's still devising new ways to kill me."

"Nah," Patrick grunted, his fingers already flying over his screen. "Got it covered, but one of us should probably go in there and assess the damage."

Speaking before I thought about my words, I said, "I'll go." I shrugged out of my suit coat, unknotted my tie, and rolled up my sleeves. "You're all paying for my dry cleaning if this ends poorly, though."

"That's no problem," Patrick said. "I figured you'd want the whole suit replaced. We're getting off cheap with dry cleaning."

Shannon was slumped against the wall, her legs drawn up and her hands resting on her knees. Her ponytail was askew, her mascara was smudged, and she barely lifted an eyelid when I closed the door and settled on the floor across from her.

"You might want to vacate the premises," she said. "My aim is bad and the splash zone is wide."

I tossed her a roll of paper towels from under the sink. "What's the deal here? What are we working with? Stomach flu? Another case of listeria in the office? What?"

Shannon pressed her palms to her eyelids and sighed. "Fetus," she murmured.

I blinked at her, convinced that I'd misheard. "Excuse me?"

"Fetus," she repeated. "I'm pregnant."

She patted her belly, and I realized she was wearing leggings, a belted tunic, and riding boots—not her usual office attire.

"I thought Andy and I had the same stomach bug, but then it turned out she had food poisoning. Will dragged me to the doctor last week, and surprise!"

"Were you..." I struggled to find the right word. Shan and I used to talk about *everything*, but our worlds were different now. This territory was murky. "Were you trying?"

She shook her head, her eyes still closed. "Nope. And before you ask, yes, I was on the pill. My husband is *very* proud of himself for accomplishing that feat."

My surge of jealousy was not small, and I felt like an asshole for it. But I wanted me and Tiel to be making a similar announcement right now, and not because we were checking off boxes or needed a new activity to entertain ourselves. We wanted to give our kids the kind of unrelenting love and acceptance that was missing from our childhoods, and build a family over the wreckages of our own.

"Will things ever be good with us again?" Shannon asked, breaking me out of my thoughts.

"What?" I asked, confused. "I'm sorry, I was—"

"I know," she interrupted. "You were somewhere else, and I was working on not vomiting, and it hit me that I'm having a baby, and we're sitting here, together, but we can't even talk. We don't talk anymore. Not really." She rolled up her sleeves and loosened her collar. "I know we both needed to grow, and that required space and distance. I get that, but sometimes I think we grew so far apart that we don't know each other anymore. I'm closer with your wife than I am with you, and even though I love her, I don't see that much of her. I'm a little heartbroken about this state of affairs right now."

She wasn't wrong. "Okay," I said. "We're not avoiding you. Things have been...busy."

"It's funny how that's your excuse now," Shannon said. "We used to work seventy, eighty hour weeks and still managed to talk every day. We're not *busy*, Sam. This operation is finally under control, and we don't spend every waking minute working to keep the wheels on anymore. It's not about being busy. You shut me out a long time ago, and even though you think you've reopened that door, you haven't. We're strangers, and I fucking hate it."

"You want to talk? Let's talk. Maybe we should start with your sudden marriage, or your *years-long* secret relationship with Will? Yeah, let's talk about that. Tell me how I shut you out with that one."

"How about *your* sudden marriage? Or how about the time when you spent three fucking months in the wilderness, and didn't once call, text, or drop a damn postcard in the mail?"

"You eloped to get back at me?" I asked.

"No, you dickhead, we eloped because we wanted to," she said. "Not everything is about you."

"And there you go," I said, gesturing toward her. "Going to Maine had nothing to do with you and everything to do with me dealing with my shit. Could I have done a better job of staying in touch? Yes. Did I need to disconnect from everything? *Hell* yes."

She scrubbed her hands over her face with a sigh. "I don't want it to be like this," she whispered. "We need to get out of survival mode. We've been running as fast and as far as possible, and we've been running so long that we don't even realize we're still doing it. We don't have to run away anymore."

"That's why I needed to leave, Shan," I said. "I couldn't do it *and* be here."

"It felt like I failed," she said. "It felt like I let you go over the edge while I did nothing to stop it, and every damn day I wondered whether you were still alive. I knew it had to be bad for you to leave like that, and all I could think was that you'd gone into the woods to kill yourself and I couldn't do a fucking thing to stop it."

Shannon balled up the paper towels she was holding and tossed them across the room.

"Then, when you came back, you went to Tiel." She held up her hands before I could object. "I love your wife, Sam. *Love her*. But you went to her first, and you've been holding us at a distance since. It's like you still aren't sure whether you want us around, and I don't want it to be like that. I want us—all of us—to be okay."

She ended that statement by puking and gagging for several unpleasant minutes where I considered the possibility that I was also a sympathetic vomiter. When she finally dropped back to the floor and thunked her head against the wall, I handed her another wad of paper towels.

"I think we're getting there," I said. "We're on our way to okay."

"I really hope so, Sam, because this kid," she started, her hand on her belly, "needs a big, noisy, messy, crazy family."

Nodding, I asked, "When are you going to share this news with the rest of the tribe?"

"Soon," she said. "It's not like I can keep it to myself much longer. I woke up yesterday morning and nothing fit. I mean *nothing*. I feel like an overstuffed sausage in these leggings." She held up her palms and shrugged. "But this was quite the shock, and we needed a minute to digest, just the two of us."

"Tiel and I…we've been trying," I said.

Shannon peeked at me for a quick second. "How's that going?"

I nodded, knowing that Tiel and I were due for a conversation on this topic. We'd been tap dancing around it for months now, quietly hoping the stars would align and we'd get lucky one of these months.

"I have no complaints about the *trying* element, but we have yet to see any success."

She blew out several breaths before responding. "Don't stress about that shit," she said. "I know that is easier said than done, and it's probably obnoxious hearing that from someone who got knocked up without trying, but give it time."

"A lot easier said than done," I laughed.

"Really, though," she said. "That kid is going to be so lucky to have you and Tiel. You're going to be the best parents, and I can't wait for that to happen."

"I have to admit, Shannon, I'm a little shocked to hear that. Where are the words of caution? Why aren't you asking about my medical issues or recommending genetic counseling? What about...I don't know, there has to be something else you're dying to say."

She rubbed her belly again, and her sick grimace tipped into a smile.

"I'm kind of dying for a pregnant friend actually, and Tiel would be an awesome pregnant friend. She wouldn't guilt anyone into going to the gym, and the absolute last place I want to be right now is the gym. She already has a million cute, flowy dresses and skirts that she'd look like the most adorable pregnant lady in the universe, and I know she'd happily share them, too. I might have to borrow some soon. And despite the fact I was a pain in your ass about her, I truly love Tiel. She's good people, and she's the best people for you."

"Oh..." I straightened my watch and brushed my thumb over the palm of my hand. "She would," I said. "She'd bring half of her closet to your place today if you asked. She'd do anything to help you out, and she just wants you to like her. Or, more specifically, not hate her."

"Tiel and I have had some colorful moments but I think we understand each other now. And believe me, it's going to happen for you guys," she said. "My little Froggie and your little band geek are going to be best buddies. Just wait, Will is going to be presiding over crawling races on my lawn next summer. We just need to get Matt and Lauren on this, too. But not Patrick and Andy. They're playing a twelve-year-long chess game."

"Chess game?" I repeated.

Shannon's eyes drooped shut again and she nodded. "A long chess game," she said. "Let's just say they're watching each other's moves rather carefully."

Will's voice rumbled from the conference room, and the muffled sounds of him and Patrick talking floated through the bathroom door.

"He's gonna yell at me," Shannon said. "I got a big speech this morning about needing to slow down and get more rest and wearing sensible shoes, and I told him to suck my dick while he shoved his paternalistic advice up his ass. I mean, fuck, I wore the flats but only because they go with this look. I'm not a leggings-and-heels girl."

I stood and stepped toward the door then paused, turning back to Shannon.

"Thank you for…" I started, gesturing toward her. "For this. For everything. I've been hard on you for a long time. I'm sorry. You didn't deserve all the shit I left at your door."

"I gave you some shit, too," she said, attempting to brush off my comments with a flippant shrug. She hated talking about feelings. "I think we needed some time apart. Maybe we were a little codependent, and we couldn't take any of the next steps until we found our sea legs. And of course we had to yell at each other in a bathroom to get past it all."

"You're probably right," I murmured.

"I'm often right."

Shannon opened her eyes, and we stared at each other for a moment. We were finally mourning the end of the relationship that sustained us through Angus, through our first breaths of adulthood, through the end of our twenties. We didn't spend our weekends shopping or open-housing anymore, and we didn't exchange hundreds of texts daily, and we could no longer name each other as the people who knew us best. But we were going to be okay.

"Peanut," Will growled from the doorway, "you're coming with me, and there will be no arguments."

"I don't have the energy for an argument," she said.

In one quick movement, Will scooped her off the ground and had her cradled in his arms. "There's a first time for everything," he said.

*Fourteen*

TIEL

APRIL

**Tiel:** Ok don't freak out…
**Sam:** What's wrong?
**Sam:** Are you okay?
**Sam:** Where are you I'm coming to you
**Tiel:** Honey. I'm fine. Place both hands on your tits and calm down.
**Tiel:** I was just saying don't freak out because I walked by the Berklee bookstore today, and saw a wee baby Berklee shirt
**Tiel:** And I had to get it. But it's still early and we're waiting before this gets crazy official and everything, and I didn't want you to get carried away
**Tiel:** LIKE YOU JUST DID
**Sam:** That's awesome but I'm going to need a minute to get my heart rate back down to normal, Sunshine.
**Tiel:** We have seven more months to go. Find your chill.

**Sam:** I worry about you. BOTH of you. I'm not going to stop.

**Tiel:** I know and I'm not asking you to stop. I'm just asking you to stop assuming the worst.

**Sam:** You're sure you're okay? You're feeling all right?

**Tiel:** We're good. We had two bagels with extra cream cheese and a hot chocolate (not a cappuccino) and we're good. life is good.

**Sam:** I can't wait to tell everyone.

**Tiel:** Me too. They're going to lose their shit. We have to do something totally adorkable though. Like, those pictures where the couple has their shoes lined up and then they have a tiny pair of itsy bitsy baby shoes.

**Tiel:** Or! Wait! The venti coffee cup, the grandé cup, and then the itsy bitsy baby cup!

**Sam:** So you're saying we're going to spend tonight on Pinterest?

**Tiel:** Um, yeah

---

**Tiel:** Which part of town are you in this afternoon?

**Sam:** Whichever part you want, sweetheart.

**Tiel:** Sam. Please. Be serious for a second.

**Sam:** I *am* being serious, Tiel. I can delegate just about anything to Riley and be wherever you want me.

**Tiel:** Yeah but I don't want to bother you. I know you like your schedule.

**Sam:** Fuck my schedule.

**Sam:** What's wrong? Are you doing all right?

**Tiel:** I don't think I can get on the subway again. This morning wasn't great.

**Sam:** I'll pick you up. Just tell me when.

**Sam:** Also…what happened this morning and why are you waiting until now to tell me? Should we call the doctor?

**Tiel:** It wasn't awful and I didn't want to text you with "hey I barfed again" because we need to keep some mysteries in the marriage.

**Tiel:** No doctor. It's just morning sickness…all day. I got off without any for the past nine weeks but I really don't want you worrying about the gross stuff because the whole "pushing a human out of my ladybits" thing makes me worried that it won't be pretty anymore and you'll be traumatized and never want to visit there again

**Sam:** For fuck's sake

**Sam:** Would you stop with all that and just tell me what happened this morning?

**Tiel:** You've been warned

**Tiel:** When I got off the train at Park Street Station, there was all this hot air blowing on the platform and everything smelled like pee and corn nuts and I puked in an alley. A really nice stranger stopped and gave me some napkins

**Sam:** Oh sweetheart

**Tiel:** And then I got nauseous walking down a flight of stairs a few minutes ago and I'm kinda terrified that I'm going to vomit all over the Red Line during rush hour and even though I feel gross I'm also hungry and that's so confusing and I'm so tired and Baby is kicking my ass

**Sam:** Baby is telling you that you need to take it easy.

**Sam:** I'm coming to get you in twenty minutes. We're going home. You're taking a nap. We're having a serious conversation about your teaching and research load. I'm making you some of that roasted carrot soup you like.

**Tiel:** Oh god no no no no

**Tiel:** No carrots. Carrots do not sound like something I'm going to keep down today.

**Sam:** Ok. Tell me what you can handle and I'll take care of it

**Tiel:** Would you hate me if I said macaroni and cheese?

**Sam:** A. Consider it done.

**Sam:** B. Macaroni and cheese isn't reasonable grounds to hate anyone, ever.

**Sam:** C. You need to get over this feeling that you have to do everything yourself, or that you shouldn't ask for my help. I put that baby in you. I'm going to feed you whatever the hell you want, whenever you want it, and I want you to stop apologizing for it now.

**Sam:** And if it isn't too much to ask, I'd like to know when my wife is sick in alleys. It warms my heart to know the people of Boston are kind to pregnant women, but please stop trying to handle everything alone

**Tiel:** Wow

**Sam:** Excuse me?

**Tiel:** I love your bossy side.

**Sam:** Yeah, you do.

---

**Tiel:** I've decided

**Sam:** You're welcome to add more context to that

**Tiel:** About my family

**Sam:** Ah. Yes.

**Tiel:** I'll send my dad an email but not right away. After we tell everyone else.

**Sam:** If that's what you want, I'll support you.

**Tiel:** I know, and I appreciate that

**Sam:** I'd appreciate you letting me handle that entire situation

**Tiel:** Ughhh. It's not your fight

**Sam:** You're my fight.

---

**Sam:** So…I did something today

**Tiel:** That's good.

**Tiel:** Right?

**Tiel:** Are you waiting for me to guess what you did?

**Sam:** I ordered a Cornell baby t-shirt

**Sam:** Or six. In every available color.

**Tiel:** We are going to have the nerdiest baby in the nursery.

**Tiel:** We should get him a Hogwarts scarf

**Tiel:** Would our kid be in Gryffindor or Ravenclaw?

**Sam:** Ravenclaw. All the way.

**Tiel:** omg. I can't wait to tell Andy. She has an entire Pinterest board of cute baby stuff that she showed me at lunch last weekend. She's going all out for Froggie. There was one where they painted the baby's bum to look like a pumpkin and it was beyond precious.

**Sam:** What? Like, painted how? Is that a good idea? I don't think painting a baby is safe.

**Tiel:** It's adorable! Andy's going to want to dress him up and take pictures and the cuteness might kill me. She'll learn to knit just for our little wizard. Or do you think Riley's already told them?

**Sam:** Riley hasn't said anything. He wouldn't.

**Tiel:** I'm obsessed with the RISD t-shirt he picked up in Providence last weekend.

**Sam:** You do realize that our kid already has more than two

dozen shirts, right? Between the ones we bought, and Riley's, and the ones from Ellie…this kid is representing RISD, Cornell, Berklee, and Juilliard.
**Tiel:** We'll make sure he or she is a cool nerd.
**Sam:** Two more weeks.
**Tiel:** Two more weeks.

---

**Sam:** I can't stop thinking about your tits
**Tiel:** You are such a perv
**Sam:** You have no idea.
**Sam:** You have always had a sensational rack, but those hormones are doing nice things to your body.
**Tiel:** Remember that when I'm the size of an orca
**Sam:** Listen. I'm fucking obsessed with you and nothing is going to change that.
**Sam:** How are you feeling?
**Tiel:** Good. Surprisingly good.
**Sam:** Good enough for me to tie you to the bed and reintroduce my cock to your tits?
**Tiel:** Probably, but I'm not swallowing.
**Sam:** No, you are not. I haven't come on your tits in forever.
**Sam:** What's on your schedule today? Any meetings?
**Tiel:** Research. More research. And then even more research.
**Sam:** Fuck that. I'm picking you up in half an hour. We're starting the weekend early.
**Tiel:** I don't think getting day drunk is a good idea, considering the fetus and all
**Sam:** We're not getting day drunk. We're getting day naked,

and I'm going to spend the afternoon worshipping
your body

---

**Sam:** Shannon had an ultrasound yesterday and she has
these incredible 3D pictures of the baby
**Sam:** It's equal parts bizarre and phenomenal. It's a baby…
but a baby swimming in gravy.
**Tiel:** Ohhhh. I hope we get those, too
**Sam:** I know, right?
**Tiel:** It's probably too early to find out if we're having a boy
or a girl, isn't it?
**Sam:** Tiel!
**Tiel:** What?
**Sam:** You said you wanted it to be a surprise. I thought we
agreed on surprise.
**Tiel:** But YOU don't want it to be a surprise.
**Sam:** I want what you want.
**Tiel:** That's bullshit, my love.
**Sam:** Would I like to know everything about our baby as
soon as possible? Yes. Am I willing to wait if that's your
preference? Absolutely.
**Tiel:** If the baby wants us to know, he or she will make it
known.
**Sam:** I can live with that.
**Tiel:** I have a confession
**Sam:** Please. Unburden yourself.
**Tiel:** I never thought I'd want to be part of a big family
again
**Sam:** Ah, yes. I believe you've hinted at this before.
**Tiel:** Go ahead and bust my balls, but I'm so fucking happy

that our baby is going to grow up with Shannon and Will's baby. They'll only be about two months apart and I can't wait to tell Shannon because I know she's going to freak out and thank you. Thank you for giving me all of this.

**Tiel:** Well, fuck. Now I'm crying and I have to teach a class in five minutes

**Sam:** Sunshine. Don't cry. Please.

**Sam:** I assure you, I'm the lucky one in this situation.

**Sam:** Text me as soon as you're finished for the day, and I'll come get you.

**Tiel:** I mean it, though. Thank you for giving me a family. It's like there's a part of me that was wrecked for a long, long time, and you restored it. You restored me. And I want you to know how much I needed that.

**Sam:** It goes both ways, my love.

## MAY


**Sam:** I'm walking out the door in a couple of minutes. What can I bring you?
**Tiel:** Nothing.
**Sam:** Bagels? The ones with the chocolate chips? Or cappuccino? Anything?
**Tiel:** No. I'm fine.
**Sam:** How are you feeling? Are you any better? Less pain?
**Tiel:** Not really
**Tiel:** I'm just tired and sad and everything hurts right now
**Sam:** Sweetheart…please tell me what you need.
**Sam:** Mac and cheese? Cinnamon and sugar toast? Whiskey?
**Tiel:** Can you put the baby shirts away? I don't want to see them right now.
**Sam:** Of course

**Tiel:** Just come home and be with me please.
**Sam:** I'm leaving now.


A DULL, sinking ache lived in my chest. I tossed my glasses on my countertop and pressed my fingers to my eyelids with a yawn as the din of nail guns and workers rang around me. The Brookline property was buzzing with activity as the final days of the project loomed near, but I knew I should have stayed with Tiel today. She'd ordered me to leave, insisting that she wanted to sleep.

Shannon appeared at the kitchen doorway, her phone and water bottle tucked in one hand, and a wall sconce in the other. "Hey, I need you to—"

"Nope," I interrupted. I blinked and replaced my glasses before shoving my things into my messenger bag. "I have to leave for the rest of the day."

"What?" Shannon snapped. "What are you talking about? *You* wanted all hands on deck to get ready for the photographers next week. You were gone all yesterday afternoon, and I still have a list of things to work through with you because of it. I need you here."

I was ready to yell at her. To throw something. To expel all the grief and frustration I'd been hoarding since the ultrasound tech ceased chattering about baby names, and started murmuring to herself while she methodically swiped the wand back and forth over Tiel's belly, since the doctor was called in to confirm that the heartbeat couldn't be found, since silent tears started streaming down Tiel's cheeks and hadn't yet stopped.

But I'd abandoned the practice of slamming people with my emotions.

"The timing is shit, I know," I said, "but Riley and Matt have it under control. Worst case scenario—and I mean *worst*—you call or text me."

Shannon set the sconce down and eyed me. "What's going on?" she asked. "Something's not right."

I nodded, rubbing the back of my neck to alleviate some of the tension there. I beckoned her into the mud room with me, away from the flow of work. Closing the door behind us, I said, "Tiel was pregnant. We lost the baby last night." I leaned against the wall, suddenly overwhelmed with exhaustion. "We were going to tell everyone this weekend. At Andy and Patrick's place. Tiel had beer cozies made up for everyone. They said Aunt Lauren and Uncle Riley, and…she's barely spoken since it happened. She's devastated—we both are—and all I know is that she needs me to come home."

"Sam," she gasped, her fingers flying to her baby bump. Her eyes crinkled with concern and she reached out, pulling me into her arms. "Sam, I'm so sorry. You're right, you need to go. What the hell are you even doing here?"

I released a rueful laugh, and surrendered to her tight squeeze. "As someone mentioned, I ordered all hands on deck to get through the punch list," I said. "And she wanted to be alone. They did a…a procedure last night, and we didn't get home until the morning. I thought she'd get some rest. I know now that I shouldn't have left, but…I didn't know what to do. I don't know what to do, Shannon."

She leaned back, her head shaking and her eyes shiny with tears. "Go home," she said. "Don't come in tomorrow. I don't want to see you until Monday morning at the earliest." I nodded, and she continued, "What can I do for you? Are there any clients I can handle, or anything I can take off your plate? Do you want me to grab some carryout for you guys? Can I pick up some comfy jammies for her or girl stuff she doesn't want to ask you to get, or anything?"

I shook my head. "I have no idea," I confessed. "I don't know what we need, but I don't want her alone any longer."

"Of course," Shannon said, "and I'll take care of everything. Go."

The city dissolved into a slow-moving whirlwind of noise, color, and shape as I drove home, but I couldn't process any of it. When I arrived, I abandoned my phone and messenger bag in the kitchen, and carried water, a bagel, and pain medication upstairs.

From the doorway, Tiel was nothing more than a tiny knot of woman, her head tucked to her chest and her arms roped around her knees. Her shoulders shook with quiet sobs, and it was possible that I'd never seen her shattered quite like this before.

After brushing her hair off her face, I left a kiss on her temple and convinced her to eat the bagel and swallow the pills. There was nothing I could do to shield her from this loss, and nothing to say that we hadn't already heard.

*These things happen.*

*There was nothing you could have done to prevent it.*

*It's more common than you think.*

*Don't blame yourself.*

*You can always try again.*

I held her close and stroked her hair, and stayed there long after the tears dried and she surrendered to sleep. Then, I set out to fulfill her one request. The alcove where we'd been stockpiling tiny t-shirts and socks, story books, blankets, and stuffed animals had to disappear. As I folded each item, I was filled with the dim sense that I'd never unpack them.

---

I **DIDN'T EXPECT** them to come, but I should have. If there was one thing my siblings did with remarkable consistency, it was show up, and it took this moment to realize that I *had* been holding them at a distance.

But they didn't let that distance stop them. They circled around us.

Shannon arrived the next day, and without a word, she crawled into bed with Tiel and cried along with her. Andy and Lauren turned up not long after, and I was ordered away.

They promised to care for her, and though I still felt powerless, as if I was watching her slowly drown, I trusted these women. They were each strong-willed forces of nature in their own rights, but their love was the greatest force.

I found Riley, Matt, Patrick, and Will surveying the roof deck—God forbid anyone slipped up and called it a roof garden because Patrick was never more than moments from unleashing his loathing of roof gardens—with measuring tapes and the level app on Matt's iPhone. At one time, Riley and I entertained the idea of engaging Magnolia to renovate this area, but that had been cooling on the back burner.

"There's a lot of dry rot here," Patrick said, motioning to the old deck flooring. "I'm not seeing anything that should be salvaged. We're going to pull it up and replace it with some better materials."

"You don't have to do that," I said.

"I told them that," Riley said as he devoured an apple.

Matt pointed to the low railing that faced the Fort Point Channel. "What about some benches over here? And I think you're going to want some shade. Maybe a pergola."

"Yeah," Patrick murmured to himself as he walked the perimeter. "Yeah. Let's build some of those deep planter boxes, like the ones we used on my terrace. Cypress trees would give you shade and privacy. You can never have enough privacy when it comes to women and patios."

"I appreciate the offer, but honestly, it's fine. We don't use this space and—" They weren't listening. Will was prying up decades-old wood, Matt was recording measurements, and Patrick was scoping out the roofline.

"Is she doing the naked tanning thing again?" Will asked Patrick.

"Jesus. Yes," he growled. "The first mild day of spring, she was lying out on the terrace and bare-assed for the entire North End to see."

"I lucked out with the ginger," Will said. "She's the only person I know who wears more clothes at the beach."

"You really did," Patrick answered.

Will pulled up another plank and said, "We're gonna have a lot to haul away."

Matt glanced at his watch. "I can have a construction dumpster here in an hour or two."

"Okay, all right," I said. Building a deck seemed like the last thing I should be doing while my wife was recovering from a miscarriage, but damned if I knew the first or second things to do in this situation. "If we're doing this, we're using the right tools." I pointed at Will. "Just because you can break boards with your bare hands doesn't mean you should."

"No," Will said, shaking his head slowly, "that's *exactly*

what it means. You should seize every opportunity that life gives you to tear shit apart."

We spent the weekend demolishing the old deck, and in some brutal way, it was exactly what I needed. What we all needed.

JUNE

I LOVE MY WIFE. *I love my wife. I love my wife.*

That was the only good explanation as to why my trousers were on the other side of the room, my boxer briefs were shoved to my knees, and two fingers were exploring my ass like they were Lewis and Clark and I was the fucking Oregon Trail.

*I love my wife. I love my wife. I love my wife.*

"Try to relax," I heard over my shoulder. "Just a little pressure."

There was a time when I enjoyed ass play. There was no mistaking the taboo nature of it all, but for me, it was the least intimate option on the menu. No eye contact, no kissing, no more than a lifted skirt and panties edged to the side, definitely no repeats. That time was also marked by my exceptional ability to be an unrepentant dick.

Given that I was the one bent over the table now while

cold lube trickled down, down, *down* and two surprisingly long, thick fingers moved inside me, I was feeling more than a little violated. The urge to take out a full-page apology ad in both *The Boston Globe* and *The Herald* was great, although Shannon would beat the snot out of me if I pulled that stunt.

Also, my wife wouldn't be thrilled, and this was all for her.

There was only one problem with riding on that logic: my wife didn't know I was here.

This was a full-on breach of our total honesty agreement, but since losing the baby, my words were all wrong. I wanted Tiel to know that we didn't have to dive back into any robust baby-making activities until she was ready, that my only concern was her, but nothing sounded right. Nothing made it better.

The academic year was winding down, and Tiel had thrown herself into work. It was fully apparent that she loathed this professorship, but it wasn't something she was ready to discuss. Each time I'd ventured into that territory, she'd shut it down with an insistence that her schedule would lighten up when she gained tenure, or it would be easier when she was on top of her research and publication schedule.

She didn't want to go there, and I had a good idea as to why. It was the same reason I didn't want to tell her I was here today.

"Everything looks good," the doctor said as she crossed the exam room. She snapped off her gloves and folded them over each other until they formed a tiny blue ball. If I wasn't slathered in lube and on the tail end of a thorough inspection of my belowdecks, I'd offer a wise comment about the number of blue balls a urologist encountered in the regular course of business.

Instead, I hiked up my boxers and thanked the deities for allowing me to survive that ordeal without an accidental erection. Penises were moody creatures. I couldn't be expected to know how mine would react to this experience, and wouldn't that add some flavor to the indignity of all this?

"Good," I repeated. I sat on the exam table and cringed at the sensation of lube on my backside. "Then—"

She dropped onto the rolling stool beside the table and consulted her tablet. "How long have you been trying to conceive?"

There were several answers to that. Technically, we'd been intentional about having sex during certain times since our wedding five months ago. In actuality, Tiel started keeping track of her cycles in November, around the time we got engaged. But, truly, we stopped all forms of birth control last summer.

"Six months," I said.

The doctor nodded and tapped her screen. "How old is your partner?"

"Thirty," I said.

She nodded again. "Six months at thirty isn't cause for concern yet," she said, gesturing toward me with a frown. "But since you're here and there's a history of miscarriage, I want to do a sperm count and semen analysis, and run a hormone panel. There are some early studies that suggest type 1 diabetes negatively impacts the quality of the DNA in the sperm's nuclei—"

*Of course.*

*Of fucking course.*

*I know I'm the problem in this equation. Yeah. This is* all *me.*

"—but they're limited in scope, and I'm not sold on them yet. We'll run some tests, get some data, and see what we're working with." She started typing. "Can you visit my lab today and leave a sample? If you have time, we can get answers by the end of the week."

Medical professionals were outstanding at keeping me alive. They'd been doing it since my first breath, plus all the moments when I'd treated my body like a punching bag, and for that I was thankful.

But I hated them so much that I had to talk myself out of full-on, slobbering panic attacks every time I found myself playing the patient. I hated that I was weak, that I wasn't in control, that no matter how much I sorted out my life, I'd always be fucked up.

And now I was jerking off into a cup and offering another pint of my blood for analysis.

*I love my wife. I love my wife. I love my wife.*

"Yes," I said, mentally flipping through my afternoon appointments. Riley could handle them all on his own. "I've got all day."

A nurse led me to a narrow room that was exactly as unpleasant as you'd imagine. The flat white walls were bordered with a (badly) hand-stenciled strip of mallards and rowboats. I think they were intended to be masculine, but I didn't feel that vibe from ducks. A pile of magazines was fanned out across the wicker coffee table, and a woven basket beside the television was stuffed with porn—VHS *and* DVD. The furniture was straight out of the Newly Divorced Men's Catalog, circa 1991, and I didn't think it was possible for me to touch anything without requiring a decontamination bath afterward. It wasn't more than two meters from the grandmotherly receptionist's desk, which meant echoes of every conversation traveled through the hollow-core door and left me with the sense I was masturbating in the yarn aisle of a craft store.

But that wasn't the worst of it.

Nope, the worst part was knowing that this room was the clinical equivalent of an hourly motel. But I had to know whether I was the root of our issues.

*I love my wife. I love my wife. I love my wife. Now fill the fucking cup.*

I DIDN'T KNOW where to go after leaving the urologist's office, but I knew I couldn't go home yet. I wasn't ready to chat with Tiel about her day or argue with Riley over business or sports, not when I was still busy hating my body's weaknesses and trying to forget about jerking off in the duck room. I needed to be alone with my suspected inadequacy.

Instead of returning to the comforts of the firehouse, I found myself at Wellesley, my childhood home. With Andy at the helm, the property was undergoing extensive renovations after decades of little more than basic upkeep. Add to that the twisted, tangled vines of my father's deception, and excavating the passages where he secreted away all memories of my mother and as much of us as he could force into fire-safe lockers, and this project was looking at another year before completion.

Wellesley used to serve as a monument to everything wrong in my life, and I'd be lying if I said it didn't still stir up spikes of anger and anxiety. But now, surrounded by the light of construction lamps and scaffolding, that old, awful history functioned not as dead weight but as a breathless reminder that I'd—*we'd*—survived.

I walked through each room, studying the restoration work and lingering over memories. The closet that Riley used as his personal canvas was painted over, and no sign of impressionist Rivera, Wyeth, or O'Keefe remained. The constellation map that Erin drew on her bedroom ceiling was gone, and the tricky quarter-circle window she used to sneak out was replaced. The hand-carved newel post at the top of the staircase—the one Angus smashed with a base-ball bat after one especially bad day—was repaired.

These walls had seen everything, from the loving moments to the tragedies. They knew the atrocities, even the ones we never talked about because how could we? Which words in this language were sufficient in addressing Angus's reign of terror? I'd yet to find them.

Like these walls, the only avenue available was to keep on standing, silently holding it all up. That was the only secret to our survival, and it was what I had to do now. Even if my body wasn't cooperating, even if my sperm was worthless, even if I couldn't give Tiel the babies she deserved, I was going to keep on standing.

We'd survive. We always did.

*Seventeen*

TIEL

JUNE

**IF I DIDN'T KNOW BETTER**, I'd believe Sam was cheating on me. He was being sneaky and strange, and a touch irritable, and he was distracted. But it wasn't another woman. Not with the way he scooped his arm around my torso each morning and dragged me to his chest, squeezing and holding and loving harder than any one person could ever deserve.

But he'd been coming home *very* late every night this week, and couldn't conjure a decent excuse for it. Then he begged off sex, claiming he was tired and coming down with something. He rolled away when my backside wiggled up against his morning erection with a mumbled excuse about getting to his jobsite early today. These were lines that I didn't want us crossing again, and not simply because I couldn't tolerate one more day of being treated like a porcelain doll.

All of my insecurities and abandonment triggers were on blast, and when he was more than an hour late for the Walsh Associates gathering at Eastern Standard tonight, I was nearly unhinged.

Everyone was at the Kenmore Square location to celebrate Patrick's assistants, Dylan the Girl and Lissa Wynn, lasting longer than any of his previous assistants in the entire history of the firm.

Everyone except Sam.

He'd sent a few texts earlier in the afternoon suggesting that he was tied up with one of his new projects and would be running late, but failed to respond to any of my recent messages. To make matters worse, his siblings were equally curious about his whereabouts, insisting that he wasn't in the weeds with any of his properties.

My brain was howling at me with every awful explanation and sordid scenario, and getting louder with each passing minute. I was on the verge of tears at all times because *what the actual fuck was going on in my marriage this week*, but all of those wobbly anxieties had to stay in my back pocket until I could get Sam alone.

That left me forcing a smile on my face and sipping a glass of wine while Shannon, Matt, Andy, Riley, and Tom reminisced about Patrick's penchant for firing assistants.

"He's worse than Miranda Priestly," Riley said, his pilsner glass aloft. "You know, that boss from *The Devil Wears Prada*. But worse, like if Miranda Priestly was also a warlord."

"You know *The Devil Wears Prada*?" Lauren asked.

Riley's eyes crinkled shut as he smiled and shrugged. "Of course. I'm all about the *DWP*," he said. "Don't forget: I served under the Lord Commander until he fired *me*."

Patrick shook his head with an exaggerated sigh. "I didn't fire you. I reassigned you to Matt because—"

"Because you don't like when people ask you questions," Riley interrupted. "Or breathe, or eat."

Patrick threw up his hands. "Yeah, fine. If I can hear you chewing or swallowing, I've imagined killing you at least once."

"And these two" —Shannon gestured to Lissa and Dylan— "are wasting away because of it. Remember, Patrick, we *like* them. We want to *keep* them. Please don't starve them."

Lissa waved off Shannon's comment. "We're good," she said, laughing. "No starvation here."

"Yeah," Dylan added, "we eat when he's out of the office."

"To Optimus Prime," Riley said, raising his glass. "And the Autobots who follow him."

Our glasses clinked together when I spotted Sam walking down Commonwealth Avenue, his eyes lowered as he studied his phone and his Wayfarer sunglasses propped on his head. I jumped up as he approached, and getting out from this corner of our long patio table meant climbing over Andy, shoving Lissa's chair in, and leaping off an empty seat. The entire table stopped to stare.

Grabbing his wrist, I towed him deep into the restaurant. I was desperate for a quiet corner, or an alleyway exit, but the best I could manage was the blessedly empty ladies' room.

"Tiel," Sam started, warning heavy in his voice as I locked the door behind me.

"Are you having an affair?" I asked.

He blinked at me, and his face registered no alarm. Only

mild confusion, as if I'd asked him to go line dancing tonight or help me spit-roast a pig. "What?"

"Are. You. Cheating. On. Me," I said, and the velocity of those words propelled me across the small room until we were standing a breath apart. "You've been so strange this week! You're shutting me out and coming home at weird hours, and you didn't want me to touch you this morning, and we're not having sex, and I have no other explanation than you cheating on me but that isn't the explanation I'm hoping for because I love you and trust you, and don't understand any of this. So, please. Tell me what the fuck is going on."

"It's not that at all," he said. He exhaled and rubbed his forehead. "I don't want to talk about this right now, Tiel. I haven't eaten today. My sugar is low and I need to get some food, and—"

"Why the fuck not?" I cried. "Why would you do that to yourself?"

Sam leaned back against the wall, his arms crossed over his chest and his eyes closed as he blew out another breath. "I'm trying to figure some things out, and I've lost track of other things in the process. It wasn't my intention. I forgot to eat, and when I noticed it, I also noticed I was late for this" —he waved toward the door with a grimace— "thing, and I'd missed nine messages from you. I didn't stop to eat, or call. I came here because it seemed like the right solution to my immediate issues, but I've obviously fucked up. I'm sorry. I've had a rough couple of days, Tiel."

"I've noticed," I said. "What I don't understand is why you haven't told me anything. That's only making it worse, Sam."

"I'm just...I'm not cheating on you. That's the hardest of

our hard limits." He held up his left hand and pointed at it with his right. "And I take this ring really fucking seriously."

The door handle twisted, followed by three sharp knocks. Scowling, I hollered, "In a minute."

I took his hand and pressed it to my chest, schooling my impatient expression. "Then tell me why your week has been so difficult, Sam. I need you to climb up that trust tree right now."

Sam's eyes fell shut again as he deflated. "I went to a urologist, and I had a semen analysis."

"*That's* what you've been keeping to yourself? That's why your week has been rough?" I asked. "You should have told me. I would've gone with you, and *helped*."

He didn't register that innuendo at all. That set off all the crisis mode alarms.

"I went back for a follow-up visit this afternoon. My sperm count is on the low side. It's good, but there wasn't a lot of it."

I reached for his other hand. "Where have you been since then?" I asked, my voice soft.

"Walking in circles around my new project in the South End," he said. All that secrecy and indifference I'd been reading on him morphed into discomfort and embarrass-ment. "And Wellesley. Just...thinking."

*Oh, my prepster.*

"Okay, so...it's a little low." I squinted at him. "Then what have I been swallowing? There seems to be plenty. And those times that you go all Jackson Pollock on my tits, it's not an insignificant amount. We always need two or three washcloths."

"I love that you find so much humor in this," he said, his

sour tone laced with a laugh. "I'm sitting here, telling you I might not be able to give you…to give you any of the things I'm supposed to, and you're fucking laughing about jizz."

"Would you rather I laugh about blow jobs? Because those are funny, too."

"Tiel, I'm not feeling any fucking humor right now," he snapped, but he couldn't stop the laugh from piercing his words. "The only thing I could think this week was that I didn't know what I'd do if I was the issue. Think about it, sweetheart. When we met with your doctor, after we lost the baby, she said all of your tests looked normal. You're fine. *It's me.* I'm the problem."

"Sam," I sighed, pressing my forehead to his. "Don't you remember how I found you?"

"You hypnotized me with that ankle bracelet, the one with the little bells, and you forced me into a malfunctioning elevator," he said.

"That's right, and that's because I was meant to find you. Fate, gravity, divine intervention, jingly ankle bracelets—whatever you want to call it—put you in that elevator with me," I said. "When we are meant to have a baby, we will have a baby. It might not be this month or next, or even this year, but when it happens, it will be right."

"What if we're meant to have that baby *now*, and my short sperm count is getting in the way?" he asked.

"Then let's figure out which weird-ass juices you should drink to get some action down there," I said, and his brow arched at my endorsement of his raw juice fanaticism. "Or maybe I should massage your balls but I really don't like the idea of sucking them. Oh, and Andy likes an acupuncturist in Framingham, although she says he yelled at her in broken English the whole time she was there. Maybe that's part of the treatment."

Sam pressed his fist to his mouth, but it didn't stifle his laughter. "That's it?" he asked. "I have weaksauce sperm, and you're going to massage my balls and hope for the best?"

"Yeah," I said slowly. "I want us to have tiny humans, and if your balls need some extra love and attention, I'll happily provide it for them. But..." I paused, and looked up to meet his eyes. "I don't want this to be the only thing in our lives."

"Really? I've seen your tablet, sweetheart," he said. "All the earthy-crunchy natural pregnancy books. The prenatal nutrition ones. I've even read a few of them."

"You creep on *all* my stuff, don't you?"

"I would *never* do anything like that," he said. "But let's go back to the total honesty for a minute. What if it doesn't happen for us?"

I stared at his gingham shirt. I didn't want to think about that. It was easier to believe that we would have a family, but that we weren't among the ones who got lucky on the first few tries.

A knock echoed through the little room, and Sam yelled, "In a minute."

"What if we give it a year?" I asked. "One year, and if we haven't had any luck on our own, we go back to the doctors. We explore fertility treatments, and adoption, and all the other options."

"Really?" he asked. "Just wait and see?"

"Yeah, we need to wait and see," I said, "because you were stressing about this so hard that you went to a urologist on your own and spent the week beating yourself up about your lumberjack sperm, and that meant I spent the week imagining all the terrible things that could be going on, and all of that hurts my heart. We can't do that again."

Sam cupped my face and tilted me up to meet his eyes. "I'm really thrilled that you didn't say beating myself *off*."

"I thought it," I said.

"Oh, I know you did." Sam laughed. He brought his lips to mine for the first real, non-forced kiss we'd shared all week.

"I hate that you were struggling and you didn't tell me," I mumbled against his jaw. "You should have told me about this. I would have gone with you."

"No," he cried, rearing back and pinning me with wide, alarmed eyes. "*No*. That's not the kind of appointment a husband and wife should share. And you would have tried talking me out of it, and we never would've known that the lumberjack sperm were in limited supply."

"But you're not allowed to keep this shit to yourself, Sam. Look what happens. You get all dark and moody, and fail to eat for an entire day." I pulled his blood glucose monitor from his pocket and scowled at the low reading. "This is not okay."

"I know that I violated the laws of the trust tree. Believe me when I say I didn't enjoy keeping it from you. And now that we've dealt with the issues I didn't want to discuss" — he looked down at his lap and gave his crotch a pointed frown— "we're going to deal with the issues *you* don't want to discuss."

Oh, shit. He knew. I'd been off my 'pretend everything at work is great' game since the end of the semester brought a flood of grade-grubbing undergrads to my office, and my department chair had been dropping none too subtle hints about my dearth of published papers, and now Sam knew all about my failure, too.

"What would that be?" I asked with all the innocence I could muster.

"You hate your job," he said.

"No, I don't," I said.

Another knock at the door. Simultaneously, we called, *"In a minute."*

"Yes, Sunshine, you do," he argued. "You might be the only person who doesn't know it. Now, I was surprised when you picked that gig last summer. You've never loved academia, and you had incredible offers to work directly with special needs children, and I still don't understand why you passed them up."

"Because those weren't responsible jobs," I said, exasperated. "Those were short-term fellowships or experimental initiatives, and it was time for me to have a stable job. The kind that came with health insurance and retirement plans and growth opportunities, and…important shit like that."

"Why?"

I rolled my eyes at his question. "Because you've always had a real, professional career, and I didn't want to be the same old flaky grad student girlfriend anymore. I wanted to be taken seriously."

"You are serious as sin, Tiel. You are too fucking brilliant and talented to be taken any other way," he said. "And yeah, things are going well for me, which means you have even more reason to take on the experiments and short-term programs."

"How?"

"How are you still asking me that?" he said. "I want you to lean on me. I don't want you to worry about money or health insurance or anything other than doing things that give you joy."

"You secretly crave a 1950s housewife, don't you?"

"But sweetheart, how can I not? You are fucking hot in those vintage dresses." Sam laughed, but his expression quickly turned stern. "Is it possible that you swung a little too hard on the stable job side?"

I nodded. "I guess so."

"Fuck stable. Do what you love, and it will work out. Maybe then, when you aren't up to your elbows in whiny undergrads and college politics, your body will be happier about my lumberjack sperm."

"You know what they say about lumberjacks: they *are* loners." I nestled my head against Sam's chest for a moment, pausing to breathe in and out, and forcing all the hollow jealousy, abandonment, and stress from my mind. "They're probably wondering what happened to us," I said.

"Unlikely. They probably think we're having sex in here."

Glancing up at him, I asked, "That's not something you'd want, right? We're not great at the stand-up sex thing, and I know for a fact that if you touch my panties, you'll rip them off, and afterward, I'm a walking wet spot and that isn't fun."

"You know how I feel about public restrooms," he said. "I'm not sure how I survived this conversation, but now that you have me thinking about your panties, I would like to take you home and fuck you for the next three hours. I have to make up for this week."

*Eighteen*
TIEL

**September**

THE LAST SUMMERY days of the year were surrendering to autumn, and the life Sam and I had defined for ourselves was shifting.

I'd resigned from the college at the end of the spring semester, and now I was splitting my time between starting up the early elementary orchestra program at Lauren's school and private music therapy sessions, plus the occasional guest lecture at the college. Breaking away from the hamster wheel of higher education was an immediate relief, and spending my time with young children who craved music as much as I did filled me with a joy I hadn't known I was missing.

I hadn't heard from my family in months, and that was okay. Distance was healthy, and I saw no reason to reduce that distance.

Sam and Matt decided to coach Riley through his first

major project now that his star was rising and his consultation request list was nearly as long as Sam's. Despite their differing approaches, Sam and Matt found their groove in this collaboration, and for me, it translated to more time with Lauren. We met for dinner or drinks at least once a week while the boys put in extra time with Riley, and over the spring and summer, we'd slipped into a routine of Sunday dinners at the firehouse or their loft.

Sam and I didn't talk much about the baby we'd lost.

Growing our family wasn't our primary topic of conversation anymore. We stopped predicting whether our babies would get Sam's hair or my eyes, or how dark or light their skin would be, or whether they'd be musical like me or artistic like him. I didn't offer status reports on my cycle, and we abandoned the practice of "saving" sex for my most fertile days. I put away the holistic conception and pregnancy books, the supplements and vitamins, the herbal teas and essential oils, and stopped worrying about every tiny twitch and tingle.

In a way, it was fantastic that our lives were congested with family events and hectic work commitments, as it reduced the quiet moments where we wandered into the dark forest of hoping and dreaming and wanting.

But we were still happy. Overwhelmingly happy. We had gained more in the past year than I could have ever imagined possible, and in the process, we surrendered everything we needed to leave behind.

We were happy, and the only necessity was each other.

*Nineteen*

SAM

## OCTOBER

I PICKED at a half demolished veggie tray, sneering at the untouched section of cauliflower and opting for a stubby carrot. I was a big fan of vegetables, but I'd never understand why anyone ate raw cauliflower, let alone enjoyed it.

"There are sandwiches," Matt said, gesturing to the island in Shannon's bright, beachfront kitchen. He'd been kicked back across from me at the farmhouse table, beer in hand, since we'd returned from golfing at the Myopia Hunt Club in South Hamilton.

"Nah," I said. "I'm good with carrots and beer."

"That's outstanding news but I could use a sandwich and my knee hurts like a motherfucker," he said, pointing his bottle at the bag of frozen peas molded to his leg.

Nick reached for the tray on the island, and slid them down the table to Matt. "It's probably time to get that checked out," he said. "It's only gonna get worse."

"It's not like it's hindering your game," Will quipped from the other end of the table. "That course was a fuckin' beast. How'd you nail the back nine so hard?"

Matt offered a vague murmur of acknowledgement and kept his eyes fixed on his sandwich. He didn't advertise that he'd been getting golf lessons since the spring. It has something to do with his father-in-law telling him to work on his short game, and I didn't envy him. The Commodore wasn't a man whose opinion I'd take lightly.

"William! *William!*"

Will groaned into his beer bottle as his mother's voice rang out from the living room. Judy had hosted a baby shower for Shannon today—hence our banishment to the greens—and now that most of the guests had left, she was sorting through the gifts with Shannon, Lauren, Andy, and Tiel.

I'd expected Shannon to buck against the mother-in-law gaze, but instead of rejecting Judy, she seemed to be fully embracing her. Shannon was even talking about Will's parents staying with them after the baby was born. Considering that my sister asked exactly no one for help—*ever*—I was shocked and impressed by that.

"There you are," Judy cried as she rounded the corner into the kitchen. She wagged her finger at Will while clutching a stuffed animal by the throat in the other hand. "I've been looking for you all over the house. You're going to need to put a bell on this baby if you don't want to lose him. Or her." She folded her arms and pinned him with a gaze that could peel paint. "Would you just tell me the sex already? I know you know."

Will drained his beer and set it on the table with a heavy thunk. "What do you need, Judy?"

Tiel, Lauren, and Andy appeared, their arms loaded down with leftover cupcakes and pastries. Shannon shuffled in behind them.

"We got it all, Mom," Lauren said. "And we're not supposed to bug them, or they'll go back to Montauk and have the baby without telling us, too."

Judy wrapped her arm around Shannon's shoulders as she cradled the stuffed animal in the other. "At least I'm getting a grandchild," she said. "What would I do without my darling daughter-in-law?"

Lauren turned toward the table, away from her mother, and rolled her eyes. She grabbed Matt's beer from his hand, knocking it back with one long gulp while the rest of us tried—and failed—to withhold laughter. It was easy to see how those comments rankled her and Will, but Judy's tone was loaded with stinging levity and tongue-in-cheek fun.

If I didn't know better, I'd think Judy was a long, lost Walsh with the way she busted balls.

"Are you getting impatient again?" the Commodore, Lauren and Will's father, asked Judy when he stepped inside from the patio. "By God, woman. You can only hold one baby at a time."

"You know what I need right now?" Shannon asked, seemingly oblivious to the discussion around her. "I need a piece of cake the size of my head, and some milk, and then I want to lie down and watch all the episodes of *Fixer Upper* that I have recorded."

Tiel hefted a plate. "Would a tray of cupcakes work?"

"Oh, God. I hate that show," Andy said with a groan. "You know they don't get to keep the furniture, right? It's all staged. And do you know how many clients tell me they need shiplap every-fucking-where right now? They don't know what it is or why it has no business in their Victorian Revival, but they want it."

"But you secretly love it," Lauren said.

"Sometimes," Andy conceded.

"Whoa. I didn't realize this was such a political topic. I'm going upstairs and eating all the cupcakes, and anyone who can handle *Fixer Upper* is welcome to join me." Shannon poached a sandwich off the tray.

"I'll fix you a plate, hon," Judy said, hustling around the kitchen. "You go up and get off your feet. Have a rest, and I'll take care of the leftovers here."

"Can we go through the rest of the gifts tomorrow?" Shannon asked Judy. "I wanted to do it tonight, but I'm exhausted, and—"

Judy brought her hands to Shannon's cheeks with a fond smile. "Of course we can. We'll get Froggie's clothes washed, and the closet set up, too, and then your hospital bag. The nursery will be all ready for him...or her."

"Judy," Will rumbled. "We don't know."

"Okay, okay," she said, holding her hands up in surrender. She pointed to the back stairs. "Go upstairs with the girls, and I'll bring your snack."

Tiel made her way to my side and ran her fingers through my hair. She was smiling, and that was a good sign. She'd insisted she was all right with the baby festivities, but that little wrench of jealousy still twisted at me and I had to imagine it was the same for her.

"How was your outing?" she asked as her nails scraped over the back of my neck.

Nodding, I said, "It was good. Not great, but I'm getting there."

Golf was a new arena for us, and on the course, most of us were more entertaining than skillful.

"You're awfully cute in this," she said, dipping her chin toward my red trousers with little white embroidered lobsters, navy polo shirt, and v-neck sweater. "Such a prepster. I'm going to snuggle with Shannon for a bit, and then we can head home."

Tiel dropped a quick kiss on my lips before retreating, and I went back to scrounging for carrots. Will set out another round of beers while the Commodore told stories about planting explosives on ships in the dead of night and spending three weeks in the jungles of Colombia, and it occurred to me that this was as close as we'd been in decades to parental figures. Sitting at this table and talking war stories with the Commodore while Judy doted on Shannon and harassed Lauren for grandchildren was surreal in that it was perfectly typical, though we weren't familiar with typical family interactions.

But…there was one problem.

"Does anyone know where Erin is now?" I asked when the Commodore's story about the sharks that frequented the waters off San Clemente Island and the running shark jokes at SEAL training concluded.

"Greenland," Matt and Nick replied at once.

Matt blinked down the table at Nick. "When did I tell you that? She didn't get there until yesterday."

Before Nick could respond, Riley came bounding into the kitchen with his phone in one hand and a paintbrush in the other. Sometime in the past few months, Will and Riley stumbled into a conversation about art—apparently they shared a down-low affection for mid-century American painters—and Will asked Riley to design a mural for the baby's room.

He was spending every free minute in that room, and was now referring to it as his passion project. That passion project exempted him from golf with the Commodore today.

Nick held up his phone. "That's the hospital," he said, backing out of the kitchen. "Good round, Commodore. I'll catch you the next time you're in town, sir. Hook 'em Horns."

Matt tossed the bag of frozen peas from hand to hand as he watched Nick dash down the hallway. "That was weird, right? With Nick knowing that Erin was in Greenland?"

The Commodore pointed at the seat Nick had vacated. "I like him."

"Okay, so not weird," Matt murmured. "Got it."

"I need Will," Riley announced. Seeing him without the thick beard and long hair was still jarring. I wasn't used to his light stubble and closely cropped hair yet.

"Right here, buddy," Will murmured from behind him.

"Yeah, you know about hostage situations, don't you?" Riley asked Will. "And human trafficking?"

"Why do you ask?" Will said.

Riley sighed, shaking his head as he brought his hands to his hips. "My friend is in trouble."

At this point, all activity in the kitchen had stopped, and everyone was listening to the exchange between Riley and Will.

"With *human trafficking*?" Will asked. He whistled into the large laundry room off the kitchen and held the half-door open, and a pair of chocolate lab puppies scampered to his side. He waited until they were seated and their tails stopped thumping, and then tossed small biscuits in their direction. He snapped his fingers and pointed to the staircase when they finished chomping. "Upstairs. Go lie down with mama."

"Start from the beginning, RISD," Matt called. "Just lay it out for us."

With an exaggerated sigh, Riley leaned against the island. "So this asshole kidnapped Rob Gronkowski, and he's holding him hostage because he's mad at my friend."

I glanced at Matt and Patrick, and then Will and the Commodore, and it was obvious that they were as confused as I was.

"Son, you're going to need to run that by me again," the Commodore said. His feet were anchored shoulder-width apart, and when he folded his arms over his chest, his otherwise serious demeanor turned solemn. He was getting to the heart of this matter.

Riley shook his head and held his hands out in frustration. "My friend—"

"Which friend?" I asked.

"Gigi," Riley said. "She broke up with the oily bag of sac sweat she'd been dating, and she moved out of his place."

"And how did Rob Gronkowski get involved?" Patrick asked.

"Sac Sweat kidnapped him!" Riley cried. "He's holding the little guy hostage right now, and I thought Will would know what to do because this asshole blocked Gigi's number and changed all the locks and she can't get Gronk back. He's going to sell him to the highest bidder!"

"Wait. *Little guy?*" Matt said. His forehead crinkled as he frowned. "Are we talking about New England Patriots tight end Rob Gronkowski, or..."

"Her dog," Riley said impatiently. "Gigi's Boston Terrier."

"How are you always getting roped into these ridiculous situations?" Patrick asked. "Do you not notice that they're ridiculous?"

The Commodore held up a finger. "Let me see if I understand this. The young lady ended her relationship with this fellow, and he retaliated by taking her dog. Is that correct?" Riley nodded, and the Commodore shook his head slowly as he shot a purposeful glance at him. "Son, you need to stand up for the young lady in this situation. Get off your ass and find her fucking dog."

"But...how?" Riley asked, shaking his head incredulously. "What do I do? Gigi told me he lives in Malden. I guess I could ask for the address, but...then what? Do I kick down the door, and then snatch the dog?"

"Can't believe I'm saying this," Will muttered. "I'll go with you, Riley. Give me a minute."

Riley nodded eagerly. "What are you getting? Grappling hooks? Night vision goggles? A flash bang grenade? A sniper rifle?"

Will returned from the mud room with a baseball cap in hand. "No, none of that is even remotely necessary to retrieve a fifteen pound dog," he said. "I needed to change out of my golf shoes."

"You don't think we need night vision goggles?" Riley asked.

Will settled the cap on his head and turned an expectant glare toward me, Patrick, and Matt. "We don't need night vision goggles," he said, "but I think these guys want to come along for the ride. Isn't that right?"

"I thought Batman worked alone," Patrick said.

Riley considered this for a moment. "Less than you'd expect," he said.

"A safe mission to you all," the Commodore said. "I'll update the women."

"Don't tell Shannon anything," Will said. "She'll want to come along and knock this asshole's lights out."

The Commodore nodded. "You're on a beer run."

"Exactly," Patrick said.

With some reluctance, we agreed to this expedition. It went without saying that we were still harboring some uncertainty when it came to Magnolia. Tiel had smoothed things over with her months ago, and Magnolia and I had shared an incredibly brief and stilted exchange not long after that, but Riley was the only one who interacted with her regularly. For us to come to her dog's rescue seemed peculiar, but she was Riley's friend and she needed help. It was the right thing to do.

"We're like the Justice League," Riley said from the front seat of Will's SUV. "That is, if we reconfigured everyone's assignments." He gestured to Will. "You can be Aquaman, obviously."

"This is where you stop talking," Will said.

The ride to Malden was quick and quiet. Where I expected Will to offer some primer on negotiating with relationship terrorists, he was silent. When we arrived at Sac Sweat's neighborhood—Riley'd indicated his name was Cole, but we were sticking with Sac Sweat—Will circled the block twice before pulling up in front of the house.

"You go to the door," he said to Riley. "Get him talking and see if he'll hand over the dog. The rest of you watch his six. Try to look intimidating. Do nothing but stand there because a substantial force speaks power. Don't engage with this douche canoe, and don't throw down unless he goes there first. I'm heading around back."

Riley gave a decisive nod. "Autobots," he yelled, and sliced his hand forward. "Roll out."

While the four of us approached the door—still dressed for the golf course, naturally—Will crouched down along the fence and darted toward the backyard.

"This is going to be exciting," Patrick grumbled as Riley rang the doorbell. The sound sent the dog into a furious barking fit, and we listened as Sac Sweat yelled at him to shut up. "Really exciting."

The door swung open, and Sac Sweat took in our clothes with a sneer. "Isn't it a little late for you guys to be out selling retirement accounts?"

He was a big guy but it wasn't hard to see that he went for the bulk over strength. He was wearing loose track pants and a deliberately tight t-shirt, and several saints' medals along with his gold crucifix.

"No curfew tonight," Riley said easily. "I'm here for Magnolia's dog."

"What dog?" Sac Sweat asked with a shrug. Gronk was still barking.

"Dude," Riley drawled. "Come on. Give me the dog and we'll call it a day."

Sac Sweat flipped him off before crossing his beefy arms over his chest. "I'm not your *dude,* bro, and I don't have anyone's dog. Get the fuck off my porch."

*Where the hell is Will?*

Riley waved at the door. "We can *all* hear the dog," he said. "She doesn't even want the rest of her stuff back. Just the dog. You can keep the furniture and the flat screen television, and that's awfully generous with you being such a fucking cumstain and all."

"No dog here," Sac Sweat said with a flippant shrug. "Bitch must have me confused with some other guy she was banging."

"Oh, you mean this dog?" Will called from inside the house. He was headed straight for Sac Sweat, and had Gronk tucked under his arm. "We're taking him with us. Where are his toys?"

"Who the fuck are you?" Sac Sweat roared. "How the fuck did you get in my house?"

Will reached out and grabbed his wrist, and within an eye blink, he was falling to his knees and howling in pain.

"You like these fingers?" Will asked. He sounded casual, as if he was asking how he liked his steak cooked. "You wouldn't want these fingers broken, would you? Good, good. Now, get up, you fucking cocksucker, and find the goddamn dog toys."

Will followed him around the house while we stood guard at the door. Sac Sweat produced a grocery bag filled with stuffed animals, rawhide bones, and tennis balls, and Will gestured toward Matt. "Hand them over, to my friend here," he said. "What about this guy's bed? Where does he sleep?"

Sac Sweat kicked an empty case of beer and swore under his breath. "He's a dog. He sleeps on the fucking floor."

Will growled and shook his head, staring at him for a long moment before twisting Sac Sweat's ear lobe. He was on the ground and whimpering again.

"You're some kind of stupid," Will said. "I'm not leaving here without the dog's bed, his food, and his bowl. Nothing would make me happier than to take your ear with me, too. I'll add it to the jar I keep in my basement."

"Okay, okay," Sac Sweat cried. "Fine. I'll get the stuff, you creepy asshole. That bitch wasn't worth this kind of trouble."

"Shut the fuck up," Will said, "or be prepared to complete this task with some broken fingers."

"Guys," Riley murmured, glancing at us over his shoulder. "I didn't realize Will was a *real* badass motherfucker. I'm a little scared right now."

Matt snorted. "You and me both."

Sac Sweat bitched and moaned the entire time, but eventually produced all of Gronk's things. "Hopefully the search for your testicles won't be nearly as complicated as rounding up some fucking kibble," Will said. "What kind of man steals a girl's dog? You have some fucking problems. Get a goddamn therapist. Try anger management. Meditate. And whatever you do, lay off the juice, man."

That sent Sac Sweat on edge, and he rammed his fist against the door jamb. "Get the fuck off my property before I call the cops," he yelled. "My uncle's a State Trooper."

"Everyone's uncle is a Statey," Patrick replied. "And *you* stole a dog from a nice woman. You are the dickhead in this situation."

"This guy's not worth another second," I said. "Let's get out of here."

Will placed Gronk in Riley's hands as he inclined his head toward the SUV, and we backed away from the front porch. "Hey, swamp ass," he called, pivoting on the last step. "I took all your spoons. Have fun with that."

Sac Sweat glowered at us from his door, but didn't respond until we were within feet of the car.

"I knew she was a slut but I didn't think she'd run five dicks at once," he shouted. "Does she charge extra for that?"

Riley stopped, his jaw locked and his eyes narrowed, but didn't turn back.

"You're gonna need to double bag it with that whore," he continued. "Fuckin' trash."

"Are you handling this, or am I?" Will asked Riley under his breath.

Riley shoved the dog into Will's arms, turned, and within two huge strides, was driving his fist into Sac Sweat's jaw.

"Keep talking," Riley said, grabbing him by the front of his shirt. "Let's hear you spew some more shit because all I've wanted to do for the past hour is beat the snot out of your punk ass."

"Someone had to do it," Will said with a sigh. He handed the dog to me before counting to ten and pulling Riley away. "Okay, that's enough. He's already ugly, don't make it worse or he'll keep stealing dogs to get attention from the ladies."

Riley wiped his bloodied knuckles on his jeans. "Don't ever bother her again," he snarled. "I will come back here, and I'll wreck more than your face."

We piled into the SUV, now heavy one Boston Terrier and his belongings, and peeled out of the neighborhood.

"Nicely done, boys," Will said. "It's good to know that you can get your shit together sometimes."

"We really are like the Justice League," Riley said. "Or the Autobots. Or some bigger, better, united version of both."

"How did Gigi hook up with a douche canoe like that?"

Matt asked. "She's a pretty girl, and she's smart, and he was…shit, he was a damn fucktart."

"Yeah, she deserves better than an asshole like that," I added.

From the front seat, Riley shook his head. "Oh, trust me," he said. "She's heard that from me more than once. He made her pay for everything, and then opened credit cards in her name without telling her. And he was a mean little bitch, too. Always saying shitty things to her, and making her feel bad. She believed it would get better, but then something happened, and she finally saw the light."

"What a miserable excuse for a man," Will muttered.

"Awful," Riley said. "Did you really take his spoons?"

"Affirmative," Will said. He shifted in his seat, and pulled a dial from his pocket. Wires hung from it like tentacles, and he tossed it to Riley. "Thermostat, too."

Riley turned it over in his hands. "Teach me your ways," he said, awed.

"We should work with her more," Patrick said with a note of hesitation. Matt and I glanced at each other, eyebrows raised at Patrick's change of heart. "Her gardens are…they're very good."

Riley snorted. "That's what I've been screaming about."

"This guy is no Gronk," Patrick said, a skeptical eye trained on the dog in my lap.

"You're right," Matt said. "He's more of a Jimmy Garapolo."

We drove to Magnolia's aunt's house, where she was staying until she found a new place. It was a charming stone cottage near the shore in Beverly, not too far from Will and Shannon, and the property was with overflowing with rosebushes, crab apple and cherry blossom trees, and—perhaps none too coincidentally—magnolia trees.

When she opened the door, her expression immediately registered shock, joy, and relief, and then tears were streaming down her face. She plucked the pup from Riley's hands and cuddled him to her chest.

"Thank you, thank you so much. Frannie," she called over her shoulder. "Come quick, they found Gronk!" She smiled at us graciously, and then noticed all the dog paraphernalia we were carrying. "You even brought his things! Oh, my God. I can't believe this. I was convinced I'd never see my little boy again, and I don't even know how to thank you."

Will reached into the zipper pocket on his thigh and retrieved a handful of spoons. "These are for you," he said. "I also removed half of the light bulbs in his house, and then jacked the heat up to ninety degrees before disconnecting the thermostat. He's going to sweat his little dick off in the dark tonight, and he's going to be eating his cereal with a fork tomorrow. Seems appropriate."

"Thank you," she said. "You didn't have to go to all this trouble for me. I don't deserve this."

"You didn't deserve that cuntsucker," Riley said. "Us getting Gronk back was nothing, and we'd do it again."

An older woman wearing a sauce-splattered apron appeared, and she shoved her glasses onto her head. "I told you it would be all right," she said. "That dipshit Cole wasn't worth your time, and he was too lazy to do anything to Gronk aside from being a big bully. I told you he wouldn't sell him on Craigslist."

"This is my aunt, Francesca," Magnolia said, gesturing to

the woman while Gronk bathed her face in kisses. "You know Riley, and this is Matt, Patrick, Sam—"

"Sam," Francesca cried. "Sam, it's nice to finally put a face to the name. I've heard so much about you."

"I bet you have," I murmured.

Magnolia pointed at Will. "I don't think we've met."

He extended his hand with a quick nod. "Will," he said. "Shannon's husband."

"Right, right. I think I saw you at the Turlan event last winter," she said. "We've been making spicy sausage and peppers today because—"

"—because she was making herself sick with stress," Francesca said, interrupting Magnolia with a wag of her finger.

"Will you stay for a bit? We have plenty, and I need to say thank you about seven million more times, and maybe you can tell me how you busted up your hand." Magnolia nodded toward Riley.

"Thank you, ma'am," Will said, "but it was no trouble."

"Trouble or not," Magnolia said, "I owe you guys."

We exchanged quick glances and shrugs, and Patrick said, "I could eat."

"I have enough for an army, and in our family, we show our love and appreciation with food. You're coming in, you're staying, we're feeding you," Francesca said, and it wasn't up for debate.

*Twenty*

TIEL

*November*

"LET'S DO SOMETHING TODAY," I murmured.

"And by *do something,* you mean stay in bed. Correct?" Sam asked, his chin scruff scraping over my shoulder. "When was the last time we did that? I haven't had you all to myself in months."

It was true. Since school was back in session and Sam was busy with several new projects, we'd been running in every odd direction, all the time, and we were savoring this one, glorious weekend of relative calm. Riley was out of town with a college friend's bachelor party weekend, and the firehouse was remarkably quiet.

I loved the never-ending family festivities, but I also loved Sunday morning snuggletimes. I was as shocked as anyone to discover that I liked the chaos, noise, and clinically manic levels of over-involvement in Sam's family, but I'd always assumed big, bossy families made a habit of kicking their own to the curb. That wasn't how the Walshes rolled, and now I understood that.

"You can have me all to yourself at the movies," I said. "Or that new brunch spot, the one that puts a fried egg on a donut."

"Oh, that's right up my alley," Sam groused. "But I'll remind you, we can also stay in bed all day. You've been so freaking busy that you're too tired for anything more than me eating your pussy. I haven't had a proper blow job in three months."

I sat up, suddenly concerned. "Are you mad?"

Sam scowled, shaking his head. "Of course not. You love having a million things going on at once, and I love that every one of those things makes you happy. I have no idea where you are at any point in the day because your schedule is too complicated for me to follow, but blow jobs are a small price to pay for your good spirits."

I rolled my eyes. "Your poor, neglected cock."

He lifted up the blankets, nodding between his legs. "You're welcome to make amends."

---

I LEANED against the bathroom counter while I brushed my teeth, bringing my face close to the mirror, and ran my finger over my upper lip.

The fine, dark hairs always appeared above my lip every month or so. Ellie always said it wasn't particularly noticeable and I shouldn't stress about it, but I noticed. I always envied the women who had only a light dusting of peach fuzz on their arms, and the ones who could go entire weeks without shaving their legs and not look like a gorilla.

The girlstache wasn't bad, but keeping it in check was half the battle. Reaching into a drawer for the crème bleach treatment, my eyes landed on an unopened box of tampons. I remembered exactly when I bought them because I grabbed some chocolate-covered marshmallow pumpkins in anticipation of my premenstrual chocolate requirement, and then commiserated with the cashier about the Halloween festivities starting in early September these days.

It was the middle of November now.

*Nope, nope, nope. Not happening. It's just not happening.*

I dropped the toothbrush and darted into the bedroom for my phone, ignoring Sam's curious gaze as I snatched it off the side table. He was still tucked into the blankets and sheets, shirtless and scrolling through *The Boston Globe* on his iPad. I didn't need to see the tablet to know; it was his weekend routine.

With the door shut behind me, I pulled up the fertility app on my device. I'd stopped marking my basal body temperature every morning, and I was long past monitoring my cervical fluid, but I still tracked my periods.

My hands were shaking, and I kept tapping the wrong icon.

"It's nothing," I murmured to myself. "Nothing at all. No reason to freak out."

When the calendar finally opened, I scrolled through October, September, and August, and then back over each month as if a string of red dots would magically appear and scold me for daring to think that it'd happened for us.

Even without that damn tea recipe from my great-grandmother.

Pushing away from the door, I returned to the drawer

with the bleach and tampons. Nestled far in the back was a package of pregnancy tests, one that I'd picked up last winter when I was a week late. Fate was kind enough to wait until I'd gotten home from the pharmacy for the unmistakable cramps to start low in my belly. I'd shoved the box away, out of sight, allowed myself some pity and chocolate.

I tore the box open, tossing aside the directions and grabbing one of the test sticks with trembling hands. "It's going to be negative," I said, shoving my sleep shorts down. "Totally negative."

When I was finished, I set the test on a shelf and washed my hands while humming Lupe Fiasco's "The Show Goes On," all while pretending I wasn't going a little crazy waiting for three minutes to pass. The hopeful anticipation was the worst. Those milliseconds, when visions of baby blankets and little toes and being someone's *mother* stretched on like small eternities, flashed over and over until I started believing it could be real.

I wanted to know, but I didn't.

At the end of the last chorus, I lunged for the linen shelf. I was working so hard at bracing myself for another negative that I didn't trust the double plus signs or the big, bold letters screaming "pregnant."

"False positive," I murmured, dumping the remaining tests on the countertop.

I peed on four more sticks, and watched with a combination of shock, confusion, and terror as every single one registered the same result. Lined up on the countertop, they formed a low roar of "pregnant, pregnant, pregnant, pregnant, pregnant."

It wasn't clear how long I stood there, staring at the tests with my fingers pressed to my lips, but I jumped out of my skin when Sam called, "Everything okay in there?"

I opened the door and leaned against the jamb, my arm banded under my breasts. He was still in bed, still shirtless and sleep-rumpled, and I smiled.

"What?" he asked. He patted the empty space beside him, his eyes a little drowsy, a little heated, a little hungry. "What's the smile about?"

I pulled my lip between my teeth. "I think I'm, uh," I stammered. "I think I'm pregnant. I think we're having a baby."

Sam shot up, his tablet clattering to the ground and the blankets pooling at his waist. His gaze went from Sunday morning sexy to serious. "What? What do you mean? I know, but what—or, when? How long? Are you sure? I mean—"

"Eleven weeks. Maybe twelve. I don't know exactly. I must have lost track," I said. I pointed over my shoulder, toward the bathroom. "I'm not sure but I just took five tests and they're all positive and I think…I think we're having a baby. But it's still early. Anything could happen."

Sam vaulted out of the bed and towed me into the bathroom. I watched as his eyes raked over the row of positives. He turned to face me, his expression at once soft and wild, and he brought his hands to my cheeks.

"Tiel," he whispered, his lips pressed to my forehead. His hands shifted to my shoulders, down my arms, and settled on my waist. He dropped to his knees, pushed my t-shirt up, and ran his palm between my hips. His eyes were bright, and it wasn't until that exact moment that I felt the gravity of all those double positives. "Will you ever stop surprising me?"

"It was a surprise to me, too," I said. I dragged my fingers through his hair and canted his head to meet my eyes. "It's still early."

"Don't do that." Sam wrapped his arms around my waist, his face pressed to my belly. "It's early, but it's not *that* early."

# Twenty-One

SAM

*November*

## THE WAITING WAS THE WORST.

We were now squarely in second trimester territory but the earliest available appointment with Tiel's doctor wasn't until later this week. The near-eternal wait was torture made tolerable only by the ridiculous names Tiel routinely proposed—we were *not* naming our baby Amadeus—and Riley's insistence that he could call one of his "gynecologist friends" who could squeeze us in for a last-minute appointment.

I was absolutely certain that "gynecologist friend" was another way of saying "vagina enthusiast."

Between me and Tiel, we were doing a marvelous job at freaking the fuck out over every tiny thing, too. We debated whether we were tempting fate by adding to the baby t-shirt collection or sketching designs for a bassinet, but never came to a conclusion.

Last week, she *screamed* for me while she was in the shower. The nine steps from the bed to the bathroom shaved years off my life but I gained them all back when I found her tracing the small belly that popped seemingly overnight.

Then, in a fit of panic after Tiel slept on and off for an entire weekend, I reached out to Nick for his expert opinion.

He assured me Tiel's doctor was thorough and worth the wait. "That's who I'd want treating my wife," he said. "But listen to me, man—*do not* lose your shit. Do not get on the internet and read terrible things from Doctor Google. Do not hover around her and piss yourself about everything she eats, says, or does. Do not show her that you're off your rocker, because you need to be the level-headed one here."

"I'm not *off my rocker*," I snapped.

"Fuck yes, you are," he drawled. "You called me because your wife is *sleeping*. Leave her alone. Pregnant women need sleep. Growing a person is exhausting work. D'you disagree?"

"No, but—"

"There is nothin' else to it, man," Nick said.

He rattled off all the precautions that I'd memorized from my first read of the baby books, as well as the warning signs. As if I didn't know those, too. He offered some statistics that were meant to be comforting but left me agonizing over the dark side of those numbers.

All of this rendered me completely useless at the office. I had a pile of new properties in need of design, and several consultation requests that merited attention, but I couldn't find my focus. I was staring out the window when my door rattled open and Shannon called to me in greeting.

"I need to sit for a few minutes before I go back down to my office," she said, out of breath. She dropped to the leather sofa and propped her feet on my pillows. In the process, her phone slipped out of her hands and she swore under her breath.

"I got it," I said, rounding my desk and fetching the device from under the coffee table. "How's Froggie today?"

Shannon smiled and rubbed her belly. "Froggie might be an expert break dancer, or a ninja warrior. Either way, this kid has all the moves."

I'd never seen a more pregnant woman in my life. People frequently asked whether she was having twins or triplets, and she always responded with a pleasant offer to suck her dick. Several weeks ago, Riley asked whether she thought another baby was hiding in there, one the doctor hadn't noticed. She kicked him out of the Monday morning status meeting for that comment.

She was due any day now, and for the most part, she was upbeat despite her obvious discomfort. She'd permanently ditched the heels in favor of flats, and couldn't sit through a meeting without a meal. I made the mistake of mentioning that she was eating like a Hobbit once, and she said her husband would make my body disappear if I ever mentioned it again.

So noted.

"What are you doing up here?" I asked, a vague wave toward the hallway I shared with Patrick and Andy. Aside from the attic conference room, this was the quietest part of the office, far away from the bullpen chaos of where Shannon's staff resided. "Isn't everyone required to come to your office?"

She made an impatient, snarling sound and adjusted the cushions again. "I was beginning to forget what it looked like up here," she said. "And my husband is parked in my office because he, in his commando wisdom, believes Froggie is making an appearance today, and he's driving me up the motherfucking wall."

"I love you but if you're going into labor, please do it in Patrick's office," I said, gesturing to the door. "I really don't think I'm qualified to assist in that kind of live action situation. And this rug is two hundred years old. We can't be destroying the rug."

"Say that to me while you're choking on my dick," she muttered before glancing back to me with a smile. "How are things? With you and Tiel?"

She asked some iteration of this question with some frequency, and though I'd initially interpreted it as a sideways comment about my marriage, I now knew it was her way of offering her support. She was there for us, willing to do *anything* we needed, *anytime*, and that realization made me hate the petty, self-centered disdain with which I'd once handled her involvement in my life.

"Good," I said, and I couldn't stop the smile from breaking across my face.

"Good?" she repeated. "Or *good*?"

"*Good*," I said.

"*Good*," she breathed, nodding. "Oh, fuck. Between this" —she paused, pressing her hands to her chest, tears shiny in her eyes— "and Riley's four-million-dollar project, and Andy getting rid of the Castavechias, and the work on my house is *finally* finished, I'm going to sob like a little bitch all day, aren't I?"

I nudged the tissue box in her direction. "The deal was finalized? The Marlborough Street brownstone that Riley's been sweating for weeks?"

Her head bobbed in agreement as she blew her nose. "It's in rough shape but the owners went bananas for Riley's design. Didn't even meet with the other architects they were considering. They upped the budget to get all the extras he proposed, too, because they fucking loved everything he had in mind," she said. "I mean, he did spill water all over himself during the presentation and I think he was wearing two different boat shoes, but they couldn't stop throwing money at him."

"It's his brand," I joked. "The mismatched, disheveled savant who's running creative laps around the rest of us."

We sat in silence for several minutes as Shannon worked to find a comfortable arrangement on the sofa. Occasionally she spoke to her belly in a sweet voice, and I couldn't hold back a smile when she informed the baby it was time to stop kicking her bladder and take a nap.

"I should probably waddle down the stairs now," she said. "But first—get your ass over here and hug me because I fucking love your *good* news."

———

THE WAITING WAS *NOT* the worst. It was sitting in doctor's office, surrounded by women at every stage of pregnancy, knowing that we were minutes away from discovering something—anything—about our little band geek. Only positive, baby-filled thoughts were allowed into my consciousness, but the dark ones were right there on the edges, begging to take control.

The door swung open, and it felt like our wait was over.

"Tiel Walsh," the nurse called.

She reached for her bag as she stood, and glanced up at me when I joined her. She was wearing a navy blue tunic and leggings, but there was no mistaking the roundness in her belly. That shirt wasn't going to fit much longer.

Tiel offered a concerned frown. She knew I hated these places. "You're sure you want to come along?"

"Of course I'm coming," I said, reaching for her hand. "I'd never expect you to do this alone, and I'm selfish. I don't want to wait to see our little band geek."

With her free hand, she touched her tummy. "Band geeks are all about timing and precision. This is no band geek. An abstract artist, maybe, or a little composer making it up as he goes along."

I shot a quick smirk in her direction. "Sound like anyone you know, Sunshine?"

We followed the nurse down a winding corridor, and into a narrow room. "The doctor wants to start with the ultrasound," the nurse said, nodding toward the exam table. "Hop on up."

The nurse chattered on about the weather, the girls' weekend to Miami she was planning with her book club friends, and her holiday shopping woes as she took Tiel's vitals and got her positioned on the table, and it diffused some of the tension.

"Doctor Opydo will be in shortly," she said.

Once the door whispered shut, Tiel sucked in a quivering breath and turned wide, anxious eyes on me.

"Whatever happens," Tiel said, reaching out for my

hand, "we're going to figure it out. We're going to make it work. Everything's going to be fine. *We* are going to be fine. Promise me."

I leaned down and pressed a kiss to her forehead, and I squeezed her hand. "Always, Sunshine. We'll always figure it out. There is nothing that can happen today that we can't survive."

"Okay, and don't call the baby *it*," she said, her hand dropping to her bump. "The poor kid has been through enough already, with me not noticing him for more than two months and all."

"Him," I confirmed, and Tiel nodded. "Consider it done."

Doctor Opydo knocked, and entered the darkened room after a pause. "Good to see you two again," she said. She gestured to the flat screen monitor beside the table. "Let's have a look, and then we'll get some measurements and listen to the heartbeat."

When Tiel nodded, the doctor folded the sheet covering her abdomen down. I kept my lips on her temple and her hand in mine, and I watched as the screen filled with blurry patches. Tiel turned her face toward my chest, her eyes shut.

The doctor passed the wand over Tiel's belly, humming and murmuring to herself as she tapped the screen, and those minutes were the new worst. Instead of trying to decipher the fuzzy beige shapes, I brought my forehead to Tiel's and brushed her hair behind her ears.

"Riley landed a new project," I whispered. "All by himself, too."

"Please don't tell me you want to kick him out again," she said. "I really, *really* do not want to hear that from you right now."

I shook my head. "He can stay," I said. "He's been better about not wandering into our room."

"But not better with keeping the snake in the cage," she murmured. "One step at a time, right?"

"This is going to sound crazy," I said, chuckling, "but maybe kilts are the way to go with him."

"Well, look at this," Doctor Opydo said. She pointed at the display, smiling. "Someone wants to say hello."

I looked up, and breath caught in my throat. "Sweetheart," I said, and Tiel slowly shifted to see our perfect little composer in profile. Legs bending and stretching, heart flickering, fist tight against his mouth, tiny nose. It was all there.

Tiel reached out, her fingertips hovering over the image that seemed too vivid to be real. "He has your ears," she murmured. "Those are *your* ears."

"And your fingers," I added. "Is he trying to eat his hand?"

"Yes," the doctor said. "You've got yourself a thumbsucker."

"Those legs," Tiel said. "They're so long. He's huge. He's going to be tall, like you. Isn't he supposed to be the size of an avocado? Or is it a cantaloupe? I can never keep track of the babies-as-produce thing, and how did he get so big? We don't even know how far along we are, and I don't know which fruit my kid is, and I already sound like an awful parent."

"Take a breath. You're doing fine. Baby is healthy and measuring around sixteen weeks," the doctor said. "You're about four months, and—"

Tiel brought her hand to her mouth to stifle a sob. I

brushed the tears from her cheeks. "Can you say that again?" she asked.

"You have a healthy baby," she said patiently as she patted Tiel's hand. "This little one has also been very cooperative this morning, and if you'd like to know the sex—"

"No," I said, and at the same moment, Tiel said, "Yes."

JULY

IT WAS rough waking up like this, with the sun another hour from rising, my brain slow and sleepy, and my wife warm beside me.

But one more minute would turn that baby babble into baby cries, and if he reached the point of red-faced wailing, all hope for a peaceful morning would be lost. He did *not* like to be kept waiting.

Perhaps he was more like me than I was ready to acknowledge.

Also, Tiel needed as much sleep as she could get. That was the plan: I covered the diapers, she handled nursing, and the latter drained far more energy. We'd never discussed the division of baby responsibilities; it was on our checklist, but this kid had other plans as far as our baby-readiness checklist was concerned.

This kid *always* had other plans.

Her water broke four weeks early, on a swelteringly hot April day in the middle of a guest lecture she was giving at Berklee. In true Tiel fashion, she finished the lecture and *then* called me. We arrived at the hospital without the bag of supplies I'd been carefully curating, but Tiel didn't have the chance to step foot on the hospital's maternity wing before this baby made his appearance.

Dave, or David Wolfgang Walsh, named for Bowie, Grohl, and Mozart, of course, was born in the elevator. He was in a big damn hurry to meet us, and ended up swaddled in my most expensive suit coat. I still didn't understand how I managed to stay calm through those first minutes and hours. Tiel lost a lot of blood, and Dave was small and early—just like me—and fuck, my heart stopped every time they checked his blood glucose. It stuttered to a start only when the readings continued to stay normal.

But the minute that boy—all five feisty pounds of him— grabbed my finger and demanded my attention, I was lost. Somewhere in a dark closet of my mind lived the knowledge that my father was able to exchange the profound wallop of flat-out love that I knew wasn't unique to me and my son for hate, violence, and abuse. That made Angus even more of a monster, but I decided right then, with my son wrapped in a beautiful Prada summer wool and his grip tight on my finger, that Angus didn't get to hurt him, too.

The remnants of my Angus baggage dissolved that humid, overcast afternoon. In its place was this little man, whom Riley dubbed Simba not more than three hours after his arrival. This nickname came complete with Riley's theatrical rendition of "The Circle of Life" in our hospital room.

It wasn't until the next day, when Tiel and I were captivated by the sheer existence of Dave's little fingers and toes, that we finally recognized the full arc of the path we were walking together.

"All my best things come from elevator disasters," she said. "First it was you, and then this handsome young man."

I shuffled over to the alcove we'd arranged into a small nursery. The firehouse bordered on too big, and neither Tiel nor I liked the idea of a far-off baby's room. Instead, we created space within our room, and figured we had plenty of time to adjust. We also discovered that his every-three-hours milk and diaper requirements were best met with him within stumbling distance, at least where sleep-deprived parents were concerned.

Dave waved a drool-covered fist when I leaned over the bassinet. I'd only finished building it a few days before his arrival. He cooed and kicked, and that toothless greeting still hit me like a blow to the chest, even after three months.

"Good morning," I whispered, my finger stroking over his cheek. He had Tiel's dark hair and my lighter skin, and he had her bright, wild smile. I lifted him up and tucked him against my chest, my lips passing over his downy hair. "Let's get you changed, and over to our favorite lady."

At this point, I was a pro at diapering, but the learning curve had been steep. His hatred for cold wipes was well documented. He peed on me more times than I cared to admit. There were accidents I prayed I could scrub from memory.

I snapped the University of Hawaii onesie that Erin gave Dave when she was in town last month, and replaced the socks he'd kicked off during his sleep. He'd wiggle out of them again—somehow—and I'd keep putting them back on. He didn't care for swaddling, sleeper sacks, or footie pajamas, but Shannon insisted he was a hot potato and wouldn't shiver to death. Apparently Froggie was the same way, and at eight months old now, that little girl was healthy as a horse.

Tiel was leaning against the headboard when we returned, her hair tied in a messy bun and the nursing pillow at her elbow.

"How's my baby this morning?" she asked, reaching for him.

"He's excited to see you," I said, edging in beside her.

Dave adored Tiel. Save for his hangry fits, he was a happy baby, but he was happiest when he was snuggled up against her chest and listening to her sing. Who could blame him?

"In other words, hungry," she said, laughing as his wide-open mouth bobbed against her neck and chest. She eased her camisole down, and moved him into position on the pillow. "I think someone is going through a growth spurt. I'm going to wake up tomorrow morning, and you're going to be twelve pounds and busting out of this onesie like the Hulk, aren't you?"

She patted his bottom as he sighed in relief and started gulping.

Tiel was a natural. This was easy for her—exhausting, but easy. I always knew she'd be a good mother, and I always knew she'd do it her own way, and yet I was still surprised.

Part of me expected her to balk at the deluge of family and friends who all showed up within hours of Dave's birth, hovering and opinionated. She required breathing room, but she didn't seem to mind the way my noisy siblings fought over who got to hold him next, or how Shannon invaded *all* of her personal space to help Dave get the hang of nursing, or how Lauren and Andy switched off delivering home-cooked meals every evening when we returned from the hospital, and then stared Tiel down until she ate.

And it looked good on her. Her thoughts still traveled in strange paths and her rambles were charming as ever, but she now wore a calm confidence that I admired more every day. She'd even taken her family's stilted congratulations call in stride, later suggesting that I get a royal blue and white seersucker suit to match the one they sent Dave.

And oh yeah, I was all over that. Dave's suit, bowtie, and argyle sock collections were already reaching epic levels.

Our hot-blooded boy had no use for the hand-knitted baby blanket from Tiel's grandmother, but the fact our son warranted thoughtful gifts meant that I hated them a fraction less than I did before his arrival.

Giving birth in an elevator, and everything that followed, smashed some of those last self-conscious stones she carried, and she trusted herself more than I thought possible.

It was sexy as hell. I'd never been more attracted to her than I was now. I'd always been a fan of her body—before, during, and after pregnancy—but her radiance was warmer, brighter. I savored her in those rushed, groggy moments we found in the middle of the night when the work of parenting a newborn couldn't compete with our need for each other. She didn't apologize for her unwashed hair or the softness in her belly or her twitchy let-down reflex, and I loved it. No one else would ever share these experiences with her, and I treasured it all.

I could barely remember a life before our little family. It was as if I could condense all those years of anger and emptiness and self-destruction into a moment, an inch of my life, and every second with Tiel and Dave stretched into miles.

THANK YOU FOR READING! *I hope you loved Sam and Tiel's journey. Magnolia finally finds her happy ever after in The Magnolia Chronicles, now available! Keep reading for a preview of her story.*

IF YOU'RE *ready for more Walshes, Erin and Nick's story, The Spire, is now available!*

REBEL, **runner, recluse, rich girl.**

Nine years ago, Erin Walsh ran away from everything.

Home.

Family.

Secrets.

Tragedy.

Herself.

The only permanence in her life is catastrophe.

She travels from country to country, chasing disaster, teasing fire, playing with poison. She guards against real connections, and shuns the only family she has left.

She holds everyone--even her siblings--at a mile-long distance. It's the only way to protect herself.

But she can't protect herself from Nick Acevedo.

**He's the ice to her fire, and he's willing to sacrifice everything to bring her home.**

THE SPIRE **IS AVAILABLE NOW.** *Keep reading for an excerpt!*

JOIN *my newsletter for new release alerts, exclusive extended epilogues and bonus scenes, and more.*

IF NEWSLETTERS AREN'T *your thing, follow me on BookBub for preorder and new release alerts.*

VISIT MY PRIVATE READER GROUP, *Kate Canterbary's Tales, for exclusive giveaways, sneak previews of upcoming releases, and book talk.*

*also by kate canterbary*

**Vital Signs**

*Before Girl* — Cal and Stella

*The Worst Guy* — Sebastian Stremmel and Sara Shapiro

**The Walsh Series**

*Underneath It All* – Matt and Lauren

*The Space Between* – Patrick and Andy

*Necessary Restorations* – Sam and Tiel

*The Cornerstone* – Shannon and Will

*Restored* — Sam and Tiel

*The Spire* — Erin and Nick

*Preservation* — Riley and Alexandra

*Thresholds* — The Walsh Family

*Foundations* — Matt and Lauren

**The Santillian Triplets**

*The Magnolia Chronicles* — Magnolia

*Boss in the Bedsheets* — Ash and Zelda

*The Belle and the Beard* — Linden and Jasper-Anne

**Talbott's Cove**

*Fresh Catch* — Owen and Cole

*Hard Pressed* — Jackson and Annette

*Far Cry* — Brooke and JJ

*Rough Sketch* — Gus and Neera

**Benchmarks Series**

*Professional Development* — Drew and Tara

*Orientation* — Jory and Max

**Brothers In Arms**

*Missing In Action* — Wes and Tom

*Coastal Elite* — Jordan and April

Get exclusive sneak previews of upcoming releases through Kate's newsletter and private reader group, The Canterbary Tales, on Facebook.

*acknowledgments*

Writing this book was difficult, but not because Sam and Tiel didn't have plenty to say. If anything, I ended up with far more Sam, Tiel, and assorted Walsh moments than fit in this story, but it was the complexities and unexpected tragedies of life that made it hard to find the right words. There are certain moments when writing about growly, bitey boys doesn't feel that important.

Through it all, there were a few people who were always ready to listen to my rants and ramblings, and offer constructive criticism and healthy kicks in the ass, and I know this story is better because of them. Thank you for that, Amanda, Robyn, Julia, and Nicole.

To the ladies (and gentleman) of The Canterbary Tales: thank you for your endless supply of man candy, chorizo-sized bulges, book chat, humor, love, and endless affection for the Walshes.

Each day, I'm awed by the individuals who keep the book community going. The authors, bloggers, PAs, and readers in this ecosystem are amazing, and admire each of you for your contributions. Thank you for building this community, and sustaining it…even when someone breaks out the crazysauce.

My extended family learned about the Walshes rather recently, and I was a fool for thinking they'd be anything but ass-over-elbow excited about these books. To be quite transparent, they also give me a fuckton of shit about writing "smut," but much like the Walshes, it's how they show their love. To them, I'm thankful for the endless supply of material.

And to my husband, the one who keeps this train rolling even when I write *all* night long, forget his Father's Day gifts, and force him to listen to all of my wild and misshapen ideas. If it weren't for Mr. Canterbary and his willingness to be far more than my better half, there'd be no Walshes.